Beats of the HEART

Lyrical Odyssey Rock Star Series - Book 1

CHARLI B. ROSE

Always listen to the beat of your ♡.

~Charli

Copyright © 2018. Charli B. Rose.

First Edition. All rights reserved.

No part of this publication may be reproduced, distributed or transmitted in any form or by any means, including photocopying, recording, or other electronic or mechanical methods, without the prior written permission of the author, except in the case of brief quotations in a book review.

This is a work of fiction. Names, characters, businesses, places, events and incidents are either the products of the author's imagination or used in a fictitious manner. Any resemblance to actual persons, living or dead, or actual events is purely coincidental.

The author acknowledges the trademark status and trademark owners of various products referred to in this work of fiction, which have been used without permission. The publication / use of these trademarks is not authorized, associated with, or sponsored by the trademark owners.

charlirosewriter.wixsite.com/website

Cover design by Susan Garwood

Cover photo edit by Elora Keifer

Cover photographer by svetikd photography

Edited by Nathanie Serrano

Interior Formatting by EZ Book Formatting

To my boys.
The two of you are the very BEATS of my heart.
I love you both so much.

"Music gives a soul to the universe, wings to the mind, flight to the imagination and life to everything."

— Plato

About the book

Before they can have a second chance, they have to live through their first love... and heartbreak.

Izzy

We shouldn't have taken the risk. We should've stayed just friends. Best friends. But only friends. But our hearts were foolish. I'd loved him forever. So, three years ago when he offered what I always longed for, I grabbed it with both hands. But I couldn't hold on tight enough. The beauty of love blinded me. I didn't see it coming. Didn't expect to lose everything. My friend. My heart. My art. My privacy. All of them casualties of love lost.

Dawson

Every beat of my heart sang her name. She was my muse. Without her, there'd be no music. I was riding the high of fame and fortune. I had it all—status, money, her. Until the thing I'd always wanted cost me the thing I'd always needed. Love's song drowned out all the warnings. Now she was gone. So was the music. So was my will. I was left with only silence.

What happens when two hearts sharing one beat fall out of sync?

NOTE: This is part ONE of Dawson and Izzy's story. Their story will continue in early 2019.

Note from the author

Music was incredibly important in the creation of Dawson and Izzy's story, not just because Dawson is a rock star. But also, because songs, more specifically *lyrics*, provided inspiration for several scenes as I wrote their love story. I'm a huge music lover. I enjoy all genres and decades of music, so the playlist for Dawson and Izzy's love story is varied. In addition to a link for my Spotify playlist, there are little musical notes 🎼 scattered throughout the book. In the e-book version of the book, if you click on the notes, you'll be taken to the official YouTube video or the Spotify link for a song that's relevant to the scene it's in. (If you're reading the paperback, obviously the notes aren't clickable, but next to the notes, I've listed the title of the song and the artist in case you want to check them out.) I do not own the rights to any of these songs. They are added merely for reader enjoyment.

This story picks up three years into Dawson and Izzy's romantic relationship. So, this is not their beginning. It's their ending. (At least for their first go around).

Playlist link: https://spoti.fi/2D3aXgm

CONTENTS

Chapter 1	1
Chapter 2	9
Chapter 3	25
Chapter 4	43
Chapter 5	67
Chapter 6	91
Chapter 7	107
Chapter 8	121
Chapter 9	139
Chapter 10	149
Chapter 11	165
Chapter 12	173
Chapter 13	175
Chapter 14	177
Chapter 15	179
Chapter 16	181
Chapter 17	183
Chapter 18	185
Chapter 19	187
Chapter 20	191
Note from the author	193
Sneak Peek	195
About the Author	201
Acknowledgments	203

Chapter One
Izzy

🎵 "Lipstick" by Kip More

"Isabelle," a deep voice called my name. A large hand waved in the air. I couldn't see the person attached to the fluttering hand, but I hoped it was signaling me. All around me a din of foreign tongues filled the air. I pushed through the throng pulsing in every direction. Moments before, I'd disembarked my international flight into the Amsterdam Airport. My hot pink bag bumped along behind me as I tried to get to the still waving hand.

Finally, the crowd divided as if Moses had held up his staff and commanded them to part. There at the other side of the opening was my deliverer. Joe. He would take me to my salvation. With his hand pressed to his ear, he spoke into the blue-tooth headset. As soon as I got within reach, he scooped up my bag and tucked me against his side. Even with the chaos of the bustling airport, it was hard not to feel sheltered against the mountainous ex-cop who was my escort.

"Did you check any bags?"

"Nope. After touring last summer, I learned how to pack better. You'd be surprised how much I managed to cram in that bag." I pointed to the bubblegum colored rectangle Joe comically pulled behind him.

"Good. How was your flight?"

"Long," I sighed and rolled my neck in a circular motion. "Fourteen hours on a plane is no joke."

"International flights suck. You can rest soon. Ty should have the car brought around by the time we make it through this jungle."

I hurried to keep pace next to him, taking two steps for each of his one. "You know I could've caught a cab or an Uber to the hotel, saved you the trouble of coming to get me. I mean, shouldn't you be at the arena for sound check?"

"You have an Uber. It's called Ty. Everything's under control. Dawson would have my a…" He cleared his throat. "…rear if I didn't take care of getting you to the hotel safely myself."

"No worries. It's good to see you."

"You ain't foolin' me, Izzy. I know you're itching to get to the hotel and see Dawson. I'm just the consolation prize."

I squeezed him around his waist. "You're no consolation prize. But you're right. I'm dying to see Dawson. I hope traffic is light. This has been the longest month of my life."

"You guys have had longer stretches apart than this."

"I know. But it doesn't get any easier. And with the gossip rags always speculating about what he's up to, it's hard to be away from each other." I hated voicing my insecurities. They were all mine. Dawson had never given me any indication that he was anything less than a hundred percent faithful.

Joe halted. "You know he's not up to anything, right?" His face was serious.

Swallowing hard, I nodded. "I do. It's just tough reading what they all think the bad boy of rock is doing and who he's doing it with."

He clasped my shoulder. "I know. But I can tell you, once he leaves the stage every night, he has me escort him back to the bus or hotel. *Alone*."

Though I knew what he said to be true, it still felt good hearing someone else confirm it. "Thanks."

Joe stepped through the glass door, but held his arm up, keeping me behind him. He turned this way and that, examining each person on the sidewalk outside. No doubt assessing any potential threat.

"Joe, there's no need to be so cautious. I'm a nobody. People don't know who I am."

"Can never be too cautious. If anything ever happened to you, I don't know what would happen to Dawson. Come on. There's Ty."

He led me to the sleek stretch SUV parked illegally

along the curb. Ty leaned against the passenger door, looking like he belonged in the back being chauffeured around, not the front. A wide smile broke out on his face when he saw me. In three quick steps, he swept me up in his arms, squeezing tightly. After setting me back on my feet, he said, "I'm so glad you're here. Maybe D will stop sulking so much now."

I chuckled as he moved to open the back door for me.

"How long until we get to the hotel?" I asked him.

"With traffic, probably thirty minutes. It's only about ten miles. But getting out of the airport will take a bit."

I eased into the dark cavern provided by the black windows. "You gonna ride back here with me?" I asked Ty as I perched in the doorframe.

"Naw. Got to um... discuss security stuff for the next show. But D should be finished up, so you can call him."

"OK. Thanks for picking me up, guys."

"Sure thing, Izzy." Ty shut the door.

I stayed on the edge of my seat, staring out the window in disbelief that once again I was on the other side of the world. The small-town girl from South Carolina.

"You gonna stare out the window the whole ride or you gonna come give me a kiss hello?" a voice materialized from the far side of the vehicle.

I jumped with a gasp. "Daw, you're really here?" Oblivious to the motion beneath me, I launched myself across the empty space to the bench seat lining the back of the vehicle.

A quick tap of the brakes sent me tumbling as Joe pulled into the flow of traffic.

"Izzy, are you OK?" Strong arms reached down and pulled me from the carpeted floor onto the leather seat.

"I'm good. No, better than good. I'm phenomenal. You're here." My hands cupped his jaw, needing to feel him. "You're supposed to be at sound check."

"I rearranged. I didn't want to wait a second longer than necessary to have you in my arms." His hold tightened around me.

My fingers traced his face, reacquainting themselves with every breathtaking feature—the prickly scruff along his jaw adding a depth to his face, high chiseled cheekbones, perfect Roman nose, long sweeping lashes, whiskey-colored orbs, plump lips that quivered beneath my touch, deep dimple in one cheek, lush dark hair peeking from the edge of his beanie.

His eyes and fingers were making the same journey across my face—no doubt spinning lyrics in his mind as he went. "God, I've missed your face," he breathed against my skin.

🎼 "Baby I Love You" by Andy Kim

"Shut up and kiss me," I rasped.

Wrapping his hand around the back of my neck, his fingers threaded through my hair as he pressed my mouth to his. The instant our lips collided the emptiness inside my chest filled up. His free hand gripped my hip and nudged me closer. Recklessly, I threw one leg across his lap, so that I straddled him. Pressure at the small of my back urged me closer to him. Oblivious to our surroundings, I poured every ounce of love, longing and desperation into the kiss. Words had never been my strong suit, but hopefully my body language spoke volumes.

Satisfied that I wasn't planning to divorce my mouth from his any time soon, Dawson let go of my head. He tugged on the hem of my shirt where it was pinned between us. I shifted slightly, freeing the fabric without tearing my lips from his. Calloused fingers ghosted up my side leaving gooseflesh to rise in their wake. The trip north was torturously slow. By the time they reached the underside of my bra, I ached for his touch. His thumb grazed my nipple through the cotton fabric. Instinctually, I arched into his caress.

His other hand ran along the waistband of my leggings, dipping inside when they reached the front. I rose to my knees, hoping he'd yank my pants down. My own hands flew to be of assistance. From the seat beside us a mechanical voice said, "Destination ten minutes away."

Pulling back so I could form words, I breathed, "What was that?"

"We're ten minutes from the hotel."

"That's not long enough," I whined. I was desperate to feel him inside me, filling and completing me.

"It might not be long enough for me to make love to you—"

"It's not long enough for a fu... quickie either." Wow, I was so far gone, I nearly used the word I loathed.

"No. But like I was about to say, it *is* long enough for me to send you into orbit."

"Oh, yeah, Mr. HotShot?"

"Yeah," he growled. "I might have needed ten minutes when we were sixteen. But over the years I've come to know your body better than my own. I don't even need half that time."

"Take your best shot," I egged him on, knowledge that I'd reap the benefits of the challenge in my tone. He knew it too.

"Have I ever told you how much I love leggings?"

His fingers dove beneath my damp panties and began to stroke my folds. My breath hitched, and I melded my mouth to his. My tongue thrust into his mouth in a mirror image of what his fingers were doing to my core. His thumb wrote lyrics of heaven and bliss on my swollen nub. Ripping my lips from his, I threw my head back and moaned.

Wet, open-mouthed kisses littered my neck. Warmth rushed to the surface of my skin as I soared higher and higher. And then, with murmured words of love, I tipped over the edge and slowly floated back from heaven.

"That might be a new record for me," Dawson panted against my skin as he withdrew his fingers from me.

I ground my center against the bulge in his crotch, making him groan my name.

"You're going to make me walk through the lobby with a raging boner?" he panted.

"You're going to make me walk through it with a blissed out orgasmic face. I'd say we're even."

Chapter Two
Dawson

All too soon, the tap on the divider signaled we were about to be at the hotel. Unable to resist, I stole one more kiss before I eased Izzy from my lap and onto the seat next to me. Not bothering to hide the maneuver from her, I adjusted my crotch. Hunger filled her eyes as she watched. It made my blood boil each time I was able to read her desire. When we'd first explored our passion as teenagers, she'd always shuttered her feelings except in moments of absolute vulnerability. But three years ago, when we decided to venture from friends to lovers, we were both all in, hiding nothing from each other.

"I want you *so* bad right now," she growled in my ear.

"Believe me, flutterby, the feeling's mutual. I hope you didn't have your heart set on seeing anybody else tonight."

"Just you. Every delectable inch." She smirked and straightened her shirt.

The smile permanently cemented on my face didn't even fade with the group of fans waiting outside the Okura when we pulled up outside. Flashes of light flickered outside the window. I squeezed Izzy's thigh and shifted to the partition separating us from Joe and Ty. With the press of a button, the dark glass whispered down.

"Somebody must have alerted the fans that you didn't return to the hotel with the rest of the band earlier. Sorry. You want to go in more discreetly?" Joe asked, eyeing me in the mirror.

"Yeah. I don't want Izzy hounded, and I don't want to get hung up signing a bunch of autographs right now." *Priorities.*

"Give me two minutes," he said, and the glass slid shut.

Moving back to my spot next to Izzy, I tucked her against my chest and just relished the feel of her against me. Over the years, we'd managed to keep our relationship on the downlow. Originally, it was by our own design. We just hadn't wanted to be hassled. But when Izzy worked for the label to photo document one of our tours, it had been the label's insistence that we stay out of the public eye. I'd begun to resent it though. I was tired of the world thinking I was someone I wasn't.

The motion of the vehicle stopped, and in moments, Ty had the door opened. He and Joe moved to the rear to get Izzy's bag and the groceries we'd stopped for on the way to the airport.

I climbed out, then held my hand into the interior to help Izzy. "You coming?"

"Not at the moment, but hopefully I will be soon," she said with a sassy smirk.

When she put her hand in mine, I tugged her to me so fast, she collided with my chest. "Oh, you definitely will be. Over and over and over," I mumbled in her ear. "I owe you like a month of orgasms."

"While I'm giddy at the prospect of that, technically you don't owe me a month of them. I mean with all the video calls, we certainly assisted each other with plenty of climaxes while we were apart."

Over her head, I glanced at Joe and Ty, who grinned back at me, telling me they'd heard at least part of our exchange. They'd never let on to Izzy though because they'd never embarrass her like that. I shuffled her to my side then walked to where Joe and Ty waited.

"Izzy, it's good to see you again. I'm sure I'll catch you in the next few days or so," Ty said as he gave her a one-armed hug.

"You're not coming in?" she asked.

"No. The rest of the guys are heading out in a little bit. I'm going to wait with the car for them."

"OK. Then I'll see you later. Be safe."

Joe, laden down with a handful of cloth grocery bags and Izzy's suitcase, led the way to the elevator. When the doors opened, he leaned in, checking it out before letting us board. The small box was empty. Izzy and I settled in the back corner while Joe stood formidably in front of us. With one large finger, he stabbed the button for the seventeenth floor.

"You planning to stay in for the rest of the night?" Joe asked me without turning around.

"Yes. Maybe tomorrow too. At least the morning. Why?"

"The boys want to go to the Red-Light District. I'd feel better if they went with a full security team. Don't want them finding too much trouble. But I also don't want to leave you unprotected if you're going out."

"Definitely go with them. I'd feel better knowing you were keeping them safe," I said.

Izzy turned her head so that her mouth was by my ear. "You sure you wouldn't rather go with the guys? Sounds like the perfect place for a rock star to be seen."

Most of the time she was totally secure in our relationship, but occasionally it seemed as if there were these little doubts about why I'd choose to spend my time with her. Leaving one arm wrapped around her abdomen, anchoring her to me, I ran the other one up and down her arm, comfortingly.

🎼 "What Makes You Beautiful" by One Direction

"Even if you weren't here, I wouldn't be heading to

the Red-Light District. Going there doesn't appeal to me. Unless…"

"Unless what?" Her beautiful lips turned down in a frown.

My mouth hovered near her ear, so I could speak directly into it, "Unless I went with *you*."

She squirmed in my arms at the prospect but stayed silent.

"We'll talk about it later. First, we have more important things to take care of." I pressed my lips to the sensitive spot right behind her ear, eliciting shivers from her.

Ding. The elevator came to a halt on the seventeenth floor.

Once we were inside my suite, Joe set the bags of groceries on the kitchen counter and deposited Izzy's suitcase in the living room next to the staircase. Izzy and I both toed off our shoes, a habit both our parents had engrained in us since we were kids.

"Need anything else before I round up the guys and head out?" He moved toward the door.

"Nah. I think we're good. I'll check in with you tomorrow if we're going to go anywhere." I gave him a one-armed bro hug. "Thanks for picking up Izzy for me."

"No prob." Joe pulled Izzy into a hug. "It's good to have you back."

"Missed you all too," her words were muffled against his chest.

"Hey now, hands off my girl." Playfully, I tugged her back to me.

He chuckled all the way out of the suite and into the hallway.

Once Joe left, I said, "Let's put the groceries away, then I'll give you a tour."

"Your room is big enough to warrant a tour?" Her brow quirked up at me.

The suite reserved for us was the biggest I'd ever stayed in. And I'd stayed in some nice places ever since our second album dropped to huge acclaim. "Oh yeah. Wait 'til you see it. There are lots of surfaces for us to make use of. But groceries first."

"You sure you don't want to go out with the guys? I wouldn't be mad if... you know... you wanted to go... um... watch one of those shows."

She was staring at her feet and twisting the hem of her shirt between her fingers.

"Isabelle, look at me." I hadn't used her real name in years, so it caught her by surprise. Wide green eyes met mine. "Yes, this is serious enough that I pulled out your real name. So, pay attention. I don't want to go out with the guys to the Red-Light District. Or anywhere else for that matter. Maybe when I was nineteen I would've jumped at the chance. But ever since you and I decided to go all in, I have had *zero* desire to go clubbing or partying or anything with the guys. I might grab a beer with them on occasion at a bar. And I attend the mandatory meet and greets hosted by the label and the parties thrown by radio stations. But the entire time, I'm counting down the minutes until I can get back and call you. Does the record label hate it? Yes. They want me more visible. They want me partying and living the rocker lifestyle within reason because it makes for good publicity. But I don't give a crap. We're almost done with our contract, so they can go eff themselves. Do you understand?"

"Yes," she whispered.

"Good. Now let's put these away." I gave her a quick kiss before I turned my attention back to the kitchen.

I reached into one bag and pulled out strawberries, whipped cream, grapes and cheese. Working together, we put the items in the fridge. Then I unearthed a box of expensive chocolates, several bottles of Mt. Dew, a couple bottles of wine, ranch dressing and bar-b-que sauce.

"They sell Mt. Dew in Amsterdam?"

"I had Joe take me to this American specialty store, so I could stock up on your favorites. Then we hit up a couple other places to get some authentic Dutch treats." Peeking in one of the last two bags on the counter, I carried it over by her suitcase. When I got back to the kitchen, she was pulling out a loaf of truffle cheese bread, a dozen *oliebollen* and *ontbijtkoek* with butter for breakfast in the morning.

Izzy folded the empty bags and stuck them on the shelf in the corner by the fridge. Reaching for her delicate hand, I intertwined our fingers, relishing in how they fit together like puzzle pieces. "Now for a quick tour. Obviously, this is the kitchen." I tugged her through the doorway and to the left. "That's the dining room table, I'm guessing. Or maybe for conferences. Who knows?

We're not going to need seating for eight in here. But it is a nice large surface for us to use."

She ran her fingers across the shiny, light tan fabric of one of the chairs. Leaning forward, she sniffed a bloom perched in a vase on the table. The centerpiece was a beautiful rainbow of tulips, heavy on pink at my request. With a twist of a knob on the wall, sparkling lights twinkled from the crystal chandelier suspended on long cables from the second story of the suite.

She gasped. "There's an upstairs to your room? How much did this cost?"

"The hotel actually comped our rooms this time and offered this one to me since we agreed to play a five-song set in their bar upstairs last night."

"Wow. That's awesome. I just wanted to make sure you hadn't reserved this one just because I'm visiting. You already spent so much flying me here."

"Make no mistake about it, I'd have paid for this suite for your visit no matter what. You deserve to be treated like a queen all the time. *My* queen."

She opened her mouth to protest, but I silenced her with a soul-searing kiss. Her fingers slipped beneath the hem of my shirt, digging into the flesh of my back, pressing me closer. I was desperate for her. The tour of the suite was probably going to be cut short at the rate we were going. Forcefully, I tore my mouth from hers. "Come on, let me finish showing you our little slice of heaven."

I led her to the right into the living room which had a couple of couches, chairs with matching ottomans, a large square table, flat-screen TV and windows looking out over the city. Izzy flopped backwards onto the couch and moaned at the softness of the cushions. She looked so inviting sprawled on the couch.

Yanking her back up, I grinned. "Tour's not over."

"We could take a little detour," she said seductively, running her fingers in the edge of my waistband.

Quickly, I trapped her hand in mine. "Nu-uh. The first time I'm buried in you after a month without you is going to be on a bed where I have room and when I can take my time."

Her lower lip jutted out in an adorable pout, which I thumbed gently. "Come on."

With a dramatic sigh, she followed me. Twisting the silver knob on the door set in the corner, I showed her a bedroom. Two full-sized beds lined one wall while windows lined the other. The covers on the bed closest to the door were rumpled.

"Oooo, a bed," she exclaimed and started to dive on it.

"Not this room."

"But that's your shirt right there," she pointed out.

"Yeah, I tried sleeping in the master bedroom last night. But I kept reaching for you in my sleep and coming up empty handed. So, I moved down here halfway through the night. We might break in these beds at some point during your visit. But not first."

She snatched up my discarded shirt and spun toward the door.

"Don't you want to check out the view from the windows?"

"No. Right now, the only view I want is you naked above me. So, take me to bed or lose me forever."

I busted out laughing at her *Top Gun* quote.

"Is that even a possibility?" I asked her seriously as I wrapped my arms around her waist.

"What?" Her head tilted back slightly to gaze deeply into my eyes.

"Losing you forever?" My heart ached at the mere thought of it.

Her fingers ran across my jaw. "Not in this lifetime or the next."

The need radiating between us was a pulsing, living entity that couldn't be denied or ignored any longer. "Rest of the tour can wait. I need you."

Scooping her up in my arms, I dashed up the stairs.

She squealed and laughed. "Don't drop me."

"Never. I've got you." It was more than a promise for the moment. It was a promise for forever. One of these days I was going to convince her of that. Ignoring the burn in my legs from running up the floating glass steps, when I reached the top, I turned in the direction of my destination.

🎼 "I Get Weak" by Belinda Carlisle

"Wow," she breathed out when she caught sight of the sleeping area of the master suite. "You were busy." I'd bought three dozen kaleidoscope roses arranged in three vases from a florist who hand dyed them in her shop. They were placed strategically around the room. There was also a bouquet of pink knockout roses on the headboard. And the bed was covered in pink rose petals.

"I wanted you to feel how much I love you when you got here. So, the three vases of kaleidoscope roses represent the three years you've officially been mine. I had them hand dyed because I knew you'd appreciate their beauty, and they're a good representation of all the color you've brought to my life. And the big pink bouquet has one rose for every year you've had my heart. So, eighteen."

Tears shimmered in her eyes. I carried her over to one of the colorful arrangements and set her on her feet. With a delicate touch, she stroked one of the blooms. "I'm glad I brought my camera. I've never seen anything so stunning."

"I have," I whispered in her ear as I rested my chin on her shoulder and admired her. I inhaled deeply, breathing in her sweet scent. "Mmmm. You smell good enough to eat."

"It's *Happily Ever After*," she replied.

"Do you still like it?" It was a total gamble when I custom designed a perfume for Izzy. But man, it was the perfect fragrance for her.

"I love it. It's perfect."

"You're perfect." My lips trailed across the sensitive skin of her neck, leaving a variety of kisses in their wake—soft, hard, pecks, open-mouthed, nibbles and licks. Her head fell to the side giving me better access, which I happily exploited. She gripped the bottom of her shirt and started to lift, but I stopped her.

For several long weeks, I'd had to watch her undress through a computer screen. Now that we were in the same space again, I wasn't going to be denied the opportunity to undress her myself. But first I needed to kiss her. With a hand on her hip, I spun her around.

Her face turned up to mine, and I moved the small number of inches necessary to connect my mouth to hers. Eagerly, her lips parted to allow me entrance. Without haste, I plundered her mouth, relearning every nook and cranny of the mouth I loved so much.

So as to keep us both at a slower tempo, I ran my hands down her shoulders until my fingers laced with hers. Then I wrapped our joined hands around behind her back. She moaned and clutched me tighter.

As the kiss became more heated, I backed her toward the bed. After unwinding my fingers from hers, I gently lifted her shirt, breaking our kiss so that I could lift it over her head. A flash of color and shine caught my eye once the fabric was out of the way. Delicately, I picked up the heart-shaped pendant to examine it. "New necklace?"

"Yeah. I made it. Do you like it?"

"You made it?" The rainbow swirled heart lay in my palm, a mixture of colors bleeding into one another, stunning in their chaos.

"Yeah. Something I've been experimenting with. I painted a bunch of designs on the back of some glass pieces one of my professors was going to toss. Then I turned them into pendants."

"It's beautiful and unique. Like you." I lowered the tiny masterpiece back between her breasts. Then I reached behind my head and clasped a handful of my shirt and tore it over my head.

Reaching up, she tugged the beanie from my head I used to disguise myself earlier. I groaned when she dragged her fingers through my hair, scratching my scalp lightly.

With hands trembling in excitement, I unfastened my jeans and shoved them to the floor. I closed the gap between me and Izzy. My palms pressed against her sides, feeling the silky heat of her skin. Hard fingertips spanned her ribcage as her breath shuddered in and out of her lungs. The jerky rhythm was a song in itself, the bass groove. Her moans, the melody. Our hearts, the lyrics.

I reached around her and snatched the covers back, sending a shower of pink petals floating through the air. Lifting her, I carefully laid her on the bed as if she was the most precious thing I'd ever touched. And she was. Even if I had the occasion to hold the Hope Diamond, nothing would ever be more valuable than what I currently held in my hands.

Leaning up, she snaked her arms around my neck and planted scorching kisses along my collarbone while her hands skated down to my boxers. If she continued to touch me, the tempo to our love song would be shoved into fast forward, and I was determined to savor every moment of our reunion.

Gripping her wrists, I drew them over her head. Leaning against them, I pressed them into the mattress and gave her a breath-stealing kiss and ground my pelvis against her center. Too many layers separated us. When I pulled away, I said, "Keep your hands there. Don't move. Understand?"

She nodded eagerly.

"Good girl, flutterby."

With my mouth and fingers, I composed a song across her skin—a verse along her neck and collarbone, the chorus across her breasts, lathing the refrain on her nipples so they puckered beneath the red lace of her bra. Another verse written on her quivering stomach. The bridge played on the apex of her thighs. Her pants and sighs added lyrics in a language spoken only by the two of us. With a patience I didn't know I possessed, I peeled her leggings from her body. My cock jumped to attention at the sight of her in the matching crimson bra and panties. The tiny scraps of lace left little to my imagination, but I appreciated the visual.

"Did you wear these for me?" My index finger dragged a line along the scarlet edge on her inner thigh.

"Mmmhmm. Bought them just for you," she panted.

Sneaking one hand beneath her torso, I unfastened her bra. "I've still got it." I grinned in triumph as the fabric fell away. Even though we weren't official back then, being with her as a teenager had made me a pro at one-handed bra removal. Hooking my fingers in the thin waistband of her panties, I tugged them down her legs, baring her to me. Her scent filled my nostrils, making my mouth water.

Like a mighty tree, I planted my body between her thighs and leisurely kissed my way up her thigh.

"Dawson, please," she keened. Her body wriggled, trying to bring my mouth to where she wanted it most. With one arm, I reached up and plucked at her nipples, alternating between them. Her heart thundered beneath my palm.

Putting my mouth to her body once more, I continued my song composition. Varying the tempo between long, languid licks and fast, sharp beats, I created a piece full of complexity. Her skin heated beneath me, flushing a beautiful pink, and her muscles tightened like a guitar string wound too tightly. I began spelling "I love you" one letter at a time, over and over with my tongue on her clit. I managed to brand her with the words four and half times before she shattered and fell apart.

As she floated back to earth, I kicked off my boxers and climbed up her body. Eagerly, she wrapped her legs around my waist and tilted her pelvis, aligning my body with hers. As I sunk deeply into her, I mentally blessed the day she got on birth control years ago, so there'd never have to be anything between us again. Once I was fully inside, I lay pressed against her, reveling in the feel of being surrounded by her. My body was connected to her body. My heart was connected to her heart. My soul was connected to her soul. It was a heady feeling.

When I could take it no more, I began to move. In and out. Bodies joining and separating in pleasure and love. Reaching the heights of heaven together, then floating back to Earth safe in love's strong grip.

"I love you so much," I declared, staring into her eyes as we shattered together.

"I love you too."

I'd missed the feel of her in my arms, the taste of her on my lips, the sound of her in my ears, the sight of her in my eyes and the weight of her on my soul.

Chapter Three
Izzy

Slowly, I came aware of my surroundings. Strong arm wrapped around my naked torso, steady thud of a heartbeat beneath my ear, coarse hair tickling my legs, knee nestled against my core, fingers dragging up and down my spine, cock stirring to life on my thigh, muscles rising and falling under me.

"Am I dreaming?" I mumbled in a sleep-thickened voice. Lifting my head, I rested my chin on his chest.

"Mornin', beautiful." The smile on his face was brighter than the sun.

🎼 **"Good Morning, Beautiful" by Steve Holy**

"Bite your tongue." I chuckled. "Are you sure you haven't been partaking of Amsterdam's coffeehouse wares? I *know* what I look like first thing in the morning.

Messy hair, sleep lines on my face, yucky morning breath."

"I'd rather bite you than my tongue. And nothing has ever been more beautiful than you."

Lifting his head from the pillow, he pressed his lips to mine. My head jerked back from the contact. "You know I haven't brushed my teeth in like..." I mentally counted and tried to adjust for the time zones. "In like twenty-four hours or something."

He pried my fingers from where they blocked my lips. "You do know that true love is kissing with morning breath." He winked at me.

I laughed in his face, and he didn't even flinch at the wave of air I breathed on him. "I suppose if you can't swap spit and share stale, sleep breath with the one you love, then who can you?"

He pulled my face to his and drank from my mouth like a man dying of thirst. With his hand grasping my hip, he urged my body more fully onto his. Without breaking our kiss, his fingers began playing my body like his guitar. Plucking, strumming and stroking me to frantic heights. As I reached the peak, he shifted beneath me and thrust upwards, sinking home. Pulling my mouth from his, I leaned back, pushing him deeper. My gaze flitted to the mirror on the wall. We were a work of art. His hands guiding my hips, my hands pressed over his heart, we moved to a melody sung by our hearts. With our bodies married, the dreams in my heart burst into sparkling colors like fireworks, showering the air around us with love and passion and forever. The colors swirling around me were begging to be captured with paint and paper. The color of love.

When all the color exploded to brilliant, blinding white, I collapsed onto his chest. As I was dozing, our bodies still joined, Dawson's lips moved against my forehead, "I love you so damn much, flutterby."

My palm rubbed his chest over his heart as I breathed, "I love you too."

🎼 "Never Be the Same" by Camilla Cabello

~

A couple of hours later, my growling stomach woke me up. A chuckle rumbled underneath me.

"My baby needs sustenance. You stay here. I'll go get us some food, and I'll bring your bag up."

With a groan, I eased myself out of his embrace. "Wish you had superpowers that would bring me food without you having to get up."

"That wouldn't be very fair to the rest of the world, now would it?"

"What?"

"Me having magic powers in addition to being handsome, a good songwriter, a wicked guitar player and amazing in bed."

Laughter bubbled up. "You've got a point." My stomach rumbled again, demanding to be filled. "If only I could survive on love alone."

"I'll be fast. Believe me, I don't want to waste any of our time being away from you."

He sat on the edge of the bed, the muscles in his back bunching as he leaned over to grab his jeans from the floor. If only I could capture the power and grace of it. Maybe in clay I could. All thought flew out of my head when he stood and slid the denim up over his naked butt. My mouth ran dry, and my breathing picked up.

Dawson turned, and no doubt read the lust written all over my face. With a smirk, he ran down the stairs. I eased off the bed and padded in the direction of what I hoped was the bathroom. I pushed open a door and peered inside. Jackpot. Immediately to the right of the doorway was a small sink with a door next to it. The tile was cool beneath my feet when I opened that door. The overhead light slowly illuminated a toilet.

When I finished up, I washed my hands and went back to bed to wait for Dawson. As I passed my pile of discarded clothes, I rifled through them, unearthing my phone. I crawled back into bed, settling against the pile of pillows and drawing the sheet up under my armpits.

My fingers made quick work of connecting to the hotel's Wi-Fi and logging into my Facebook account. I posted a simple, but vague status. "Blissed out and in love overseas." I declined the option of tagging my location. With Lyrical Odyssey's contract being seventy-five percent over, I didn't want to make the record label execs mad at Dawson. Soon enough, the world could know that he was mine and I was his.

While I waited for him, I scrolled through my newsfeed. After looking at the most recent happenings of my friends, I checked the trending stories. After a few moments, a headline jumped out at me. I stopped scrolling and clicked to read more.

Members of LO hit up Red Light District

In between shows, members of the hit rock band Lyrical Odyssey were found enjoying themselves in Amsterdam's Red-Light District. The area provides easy access to all things that go hand in hand with rock 'n roll: sex and drugs. As seen in the photos below, the members enjoyed a performance while partying with a few fans.

Noticeably absent from the party was LO's lead singer, Dawson Anderson. Perhaps he was attending a private party of his own. Or maybe the rumblings that the band's PR people have denied for over a year are in fact true and Dawson Anderson is off the market.

Light steps on glass pulled my attention from my phone. I set my phone to the side as Dawson came into view. Balanced on my suitcase was a tray of food. Tucked under his arm was a bottle of Mt. Dew.

"Figured you wouldn't want to wait for coffee." He set his burden down on the lounge. Leaving my bag, he brought the tray over and settled it over my lap.

"You figured right. Besides *that* has got enough pick-me-up in it." I pointed to the bottle of Mt. Dew. Holding up the cups of ice, I waited while he filled them with lime-green heaven.

Sounds of satisfaction filled the room as we both took a sip of the cool refreshment. Using a knife, Dawson cut us each a piece of what looked like cake and slathered butter on each slice.

"What's this called?" I asked as I broke off a bite with my fingers. The bite of ginger filled my nostrils as I brought the thick, spongy bit to my mouth.

"I'm going to butcher the pronunciation, but it's called *ontbijtkoek*. It means breakfast cake."

"Mmm," I moaned and tried to catch the crumbs falling from my fingers. "It's so good."

"I know we kind of slept through breakfast, but it's the first meal of our day." Dawson tilted toward me and licked my lips. "You had some crumbs."

I giggled and ate another bite and another until it was all gone. After licking the sweet butter from my fingers, I sighed in satisfaction. "Thanks for breakfast, baby." I beamed at him.

"Anything for you." He moved the tray off the bed. Picking up my phone, he handed it back to me, so it wouldn't get lost in the covers. "Anything interesting going on back home?"

"No. I was actually reading about the guys. Seems they caught the attention of some journalist last night while they were out and about. The band is trending this morning."

"Wow. One night out in the Red-Light District and the paps already found them. What did the article say?"

I pulled it back up on the screen and handed it over for him to see for himself.

"Humph," he muttered as he set the phone on the nightstand. "It's actually not as scandalous as I expected. I mean they were at a *sex* show. Those photos are pretty tame."

"You're right. No naked photos or disorderly conduct. Maybe the boys are growing up," I teased. "I'll make sure to get some *grownup* photos of them for your fan pages in addition to the show pictures the label wants."

"Maybe they are growing up. So, what did you want to do today?"

"Besides you?" I joked.

"Hey, that's my line." His fingers tickled my ribs.

"Stop," I squealed, thrashing around in bed trying to escape his wiggling fingers. "You're rubbing off on me."

"I'll rub one off on you." His brows waggled at me, making me giggle again.

"Later. My muscles need to recoup."

"I was thinking while you were here, we'd go see some of the sights, so you could get some sketching done. And we'd hit up a canal dinner cruise. Maybe go to a club for some dancing. But first, I recognized that look on your face earlier. The one that you always get when an idea for a masterpiece is swirling around in your mind. So, I think you need to spend some time feeding your muse."

I launched myself at him, throwing my arms around his bare shoulders. "You know me so well. I actually have a couple of things clawing to get out of my brain. And I need to blog a little too while I'm here. Boost my readership to make the advertisers happy. But creating comes first."

I ran my index finger round and round the ink encircling his thumb, letting the idea for the color of love piece I wanted to create marinate in my mind.

"You going to create while I create?" It was something we'd done countless times before—me creating art for the eyes and him composing art for the ears.

"Of course. I've been without my muse in the flesh for too long. Got to take advantage of it while you're here."

🎼 "You're the Inspiration" by Chicago

"Let's get to work then." I scooted off the bed and moved to my bag. Unzipping the large section, I found my camera, sketchpad and pencil case. From the small pocket on the front of my bag, I removed my toiletries. "But first, I have got to brush my teeth and my hair." I held up the pouch.

"Come here." He sat near the edge of the bed and patted the space between his thighs. Unable to resist the pleading look on his face, I eagerly obliged. My naked butt pressed against his jean-clad crotch. The rough ridges of the denim brushed against the soft skin of my legs as I settled into place.

"I'll brush your hair," he offered taking my zippered pouch from me and finding my brush. I fell in love with him a little more in that instant.

One hand dragged the bristles through my long rainbow-colored locks, while the other trailed it, smoothing my tresses. After he'd eliminated all the tangles, he continued to brush a little longer. "Your hair is so soft."

Shifting my hair to one shoulder, he peppered kisses on the bare shoulder. Then he slid us to the edge of the bed and stood us up gracefully. "You'd better go before my good intentions of letting you draw get thrown out the window."

"Yes, sir." I moved to the bathroom, making sure to sway my hips as I went. Once in there, I banished my morning breath with a dollop of minty paste on my toothbrush. As I dropped my toothbrush back in my bag, I caught a glimpse of a flat, plastic rectangle. My stomach plummeted. I popped the lid open. Counted pills and empty spots.

"Baby, what day is it?" there was an edge of panic in my voice.

"Umm. I'm not sure. Let me check my phone."

While he looked for his phone, I walked back into the bedroom with the container clutched in my hand.

"Ah-ha." He held up his phone. Tinkling music floated in the air from his phone as he swiped his screen awake. "It's Tuesday afternoon. Why?"

Silently, I held up the container of pills.

"Your birth control?" Confusion made his brow wrinkle.

"Yeah. In the excitement of packing, leaving home and getting here..." I looked at the floor, wishing it would swallow me up. He'd trusted me to be responsible with this aspect of our relationship and I'd failed. "I forgot to take some of my pills. I'm sorry."

"Is that what has you looking so sad?" His head cocked to the side as he tried to figure out what was troubling me.

"I've never forgotten before. Not in seven years," I whispered. *How could I be so irresponsible?*

I sank to the foot of the bed. He pulled me into his arms. "How many did you forget?" The words were spoken against the crown of my head.

"Well I took Saturday's. So, I forgot Sunday, Monday and today." I was thankful my back was to him. I couldn't meet his gaze right now.

"What does that mean? You have to double up or something?"

"Yes. And it means we really should've used a condom." Finally, I turned my head and met his eyes to emphasize the seriousness of the situation.

"Oh." He shifted my body, so I was stretched across his lap. "We should've used several condoms. I mean, we made love…" He ticked each round off on his fingers. "I'm not even sure how many times we did it in the middle of the night. Izzy, I'm so sorry. I should've thought to remind you." His face fell.

I covered his mouth with my fingers, halting his apology and hoping to stifle his guilt. "It's not your fault."

"It's not yours either." He cupped my cheek lovingly.

"What are we going to do? You planted a lot of seeds in me," I tried to joke and lighten the mood.

"You mean if you get pregnant?" he asked in a calm voice.

Words wouldn't come, so I just nodded. The thought terrified me. We were young. My career hadn't really taken off yet. I still had a class or two I wanted to take. And Dawson and I were rarely in the same country, let alone the same house.

"What do most people in love do when they find out they're having a baby together?" He paused and kissed my lips. "They celebrate."

Convinced I'd heard him wrong, I stared at his face. "What?"

"We would celebrate. We'd get married and start planning our forever."

"You want kids?" Probably a conversation we should've had before we ever had sex the first time.

"I've *always* wanted to be a dad. Having a family with you would be a dream come true. How about you? Do you want children?" His face lit with an internal light.

Tears filled my eyes. His thumbs swiped them away when they spilled over my lids. "Ever since I was a little girl, I imagined being a mom. Of course, I figured I'd be a world-famous artist and done with college before it happened. But I'm flexible."

"And when you've thought about the father of your children, who have you pictured?" his voice held a note of uncertainty, and his eyes were focused on where his finger traced the tattooed ring on my thumb matching his.

"Ever since you moved in next door to me when we

were six years old, you've been the daddy in my daydreams."

He breathed out a sigh of relief. "It's settled then. If you, no, *we* do wind up pregnant at any point, we'll be in it together. You'll start planning a mural for the nursery, and I'll start composing lullabies. And in the meantime, we won't worry about our future babies until they're on the way. Deal?"

"Deal." And we sealed it with a kiss. With strong arms, he set me on my feet. He slipped his discarded t-shirt over my head, then pulled my hair out from under it, sending shivers over me.

"Now, go make your masterpiece." He swatted me on the butt.

Before I immersed myself in trying to capture the sparkling fireworks of color I'd envisioned earlier, I needed to clear my head. So, I picked up my camera and moved around the room taking photos of the flowers Dawson had gotten for me, symbols of our relationship. The lens didn't quite do them justice, but I had to preserve their beauty. *Who knew if they'd hold up for the rest of my trip or if customs would even let me bring them home with me?*

From the corner of the room, Dawson watched me with his guitar across his lap. He idly strummed. His eyes were filled with love.

I settled in the chair, drawing my knees up in the seat, so I could prop my sketch pad against them.

"Damn," Dawson growled from across the room.

Puzzled, I looked up. "Everything OK, baby?"

"Is everything OK? No, everything's not OK. You're about to get lost in sketching. I'm supposed to be writing you a love song. And you're perched in that chair with no panties on. How the hell am I supposed to concentrate or leave you alone to work?" his voice was ragged with need.

"You want me to put more clothes on?"

He sat there, chewing on the corner of his lip, thinking. "No. I'll just have to suffer through it. But maybe I should take my pants off and even the playing field."

"Yes. I think you should." I'd never turn down an opportunity to see his body. It was a masterpiece. All lean muscles stretched over hard lines. Shadows and contours. Perfection.

Never one to back down from a challenge, he set his guitar aside and got to his feet. The flaps of his jeans were already flared open where he'd never fastened them. He shimmied out of them, smirked at me, and picked his instrument back up.

My blood heated but seeing that expanse of skin was extra fuel for the fire of creativity raging inside of me. Closing my eyes and drawing a deep breath, I brought the reflection of us making love earlier to the forefront of my mind. The pencil moved fluidly across the page. Long lines created a torso spread over rumpled sheets. Ripples of shadow added a sense of movement in muscle. More lines and curves hinted at shoulders, breasts and an abdomen perpendicular to the muscular frame on the bed. The bend of a leg and curve of a hip blocked the marriage of bodies only hinted at with the series of lines and pencil strokes.

Digging through my pencil case, I found the perfect shades of blush pink, orchid, cornflower, mint and lemon. Messy, sweeping strokes with them generated a tangle of rainbow locks that somehow managed to look as if fingers had just been run through them or wound them around a fist. It was hot. Then I added streaks and swirls of color to the background, bursting like explosions of love between the two bodies. The sensual melody Dawson was composing was the perfect backdrop to my work.

🎼 "When You Say Nothing at All" by Alison Kraus

By the time I was satisfied, my fingers ached from gripping a pencil for so long. A glance out of the crack in the drapes revealed the sun had sunk below the horizon at some point while we worked. Standing, I stretched my arms over my head and rolled my neck to loosen it up. Before I could drop my arms, Dawson was across the room in ten strides. With gentle hands he took my sketch pad and pencil from me.

"It's not finished yet," I protested as he turned the paper, so he could see it better.

"Gosh, Izzy... Is this how you see us?" his question was a strangled whisper.

Fear of his critique stole my voice. My head bobbed up and down. No matter how many times I created something, the first time anyone saw it, I was always nervous.

"I don't know if you've ever created a more beautiful piece. When it's done, I want it. Please."

"OK," I agreed. It wasn't like I could ever display something that was so much my heart and soul in a gallery anyway.

"Now, let's go shower, so we can go on that candlelit dinner cruise along the canals. Joe will be here to get us in an hour."

He stripped his shirt from my body and led me to the bathroom. As he maneuvered us beyond the first area of the bathroom, I was overcome by the opulence of the room. A huge infinity tub rested on a platform surrounded by mirrors.

"We'll try that out tomorrow," Dawson promised as I trailed my fingers longingly over the cool porcelain edge. "No time right now."

He tugged me into the shower, which really was big enough to be a room. The circular area was tiled with a mosaic of cerulean and cream tiles around half the walls. The other half of the walls were glass. Inset in the tile were various benches and ledges. With a flip and turn, Dawson had water cascading from numerous jets and fixtures. Perched in one of the alcoves were my shampoo, conditioner and body wash. Guess he unpacked them for me at some point.

Gently, he urged me onto the bench beneath the waterfall spray. He settled behind me and leaned my body back against his, so my hair got saturated. Nimble musician fingers massaged strawberry-scented shampoo into my scalp. It felt so relaxing I could've fallen asleep there in his arms. He twisted the handheld nozzle, so he could rinse my hair. Then he repeated the process with conditioner. Dawson and I had showered together many times. But he'd never shown the level of care and pampering he was now. He'd never washed my hair before. His ministrations made me feel loved in a whole new way.

Once my hair hung down my back cleaned and conditioned, he lathered up his hands with my body wash. Then he proceeded to clean every inch of skin on my body, turning me into a wanton mess.

I returned the favor, making him squirm beneath my touch. And when he could take no more, I eased to my knees on the tiled floor. I gripped the length of him firmly and gave a gentle tug. Pressing my other hand into his thigh, I balanced myself as I leaned forward, taking him into my mouth. I teased him with a variety of licks, nips, scrapes and sucks.

Over the years, I'd amassed a tremendous amount of knowledge, a virtual encyclopedia, on what Dawson liked best, what drove him insane. And I made it my mission to drive him to the brink every time I had the pleasure of expressing my love in this manner. He grew hotter and heavier in my mouth as I worked his length with my mouth and hand. His thigh muscles tightened beneath my palm, alerting to me to his precarious state. As I doubled down, prepared to shove him over the edge, his hands gripped me under my arms, drawing me reluctantly off his throbbing cock. It was an angry shade of purple.

"Why'd you stop me?" I pouted, catching my breath.

"You know why I stopped you," he croaked.

On trembling legs, he drew us both to our feet. He planted my hands on the shower wall and kissed a line down my spine. Pressing my back to his front, he melded our bodies together. Our hearts fused as one. Our souls fitting together as if they were carved from the same bit of heavenly essence. Forgoing any more actual bathing, we made love with the sounds of our pleasure echoing around us.

When we were finally sated, we dried each other off and got ready. Hastily, I dug out a sweater dress and leggings. I had twenty minutes to get ready before Joe would be ready to escort us down to the boat.

"How do I look?" I asked when I emerged from the dressing area.

"Stunning. But you're going to need this." He slid a black beanie over my hair. It matched his. "It's a little chilly out there, especially along the water."

"Thanks."

Thirty minutes later we were strolling along the cobblestoned paths, hand-in-hand with Joe trailing behind us. A cluster of people paid special attention to us as they passed, craning their heads to get a second look. Moments later a flash of light lit up the other side of the street.

"Damn it," Dawson huffed under his breath.

"Just keep moving. We're almost to the boat," Joe urged as he stepped closer to us.

By the time we boarded the boat for our private

dinner cruise, I'd forgotten about the photograph. The flickering bridge lights as we cruised the canal belt enraptured me. As we floated, I marveled at the rainbow formed on either side of the canal by the buildings.

"Oh," I gasped. I tugged Dawson's arm. "Is that a pink canal?"

"Yeah. When you put *pink river* on our bucket list years ago, you didn't specify anything else. Hope this will do."

"It's perfect," I breathed out as our boat glided through a tunnel formed by pink flowering trees. The pink petals dotting the water along with the tree's reflections made the canal look pink.

Withdrawing my camera from my coat pocket, I snapped images of the sights in between stealing kisses and selfies with Dawson. The dinner was amazing, made even more so by the romantic atmosphere. I wished I could freeze time and stay forever in this place with Dawson.

Chapter Four
Dawson

🎼 "Angel of the Morning" by Juice Newton

A soft warmth pressed me to the mattress. Blinking, my vision filled with color. Silky hair spread over my shoulder and trailed down one arm, almost tickling it. One of my arms anchored the presence of heaven to me—chest to chest, heart to heart. Wet heat pushed against my hard cock, which was straining to gain entry of its own accord. A minor tilt of my hips and slip of her body would easily accomplish it. But the torture of her damp folds barely sliding against me with each exchange of breath was delicious and worth savoring. Her knees squeezed my hips as her long legs lay alongside my own. The fingers of her hand resting on my pec twitched and flexed. She was beginning to wake up. With my free hand, I dragged my fingers through her hair.

Her lashes fluttered where they rested against my skin.

"Hey, you," I spoke quietly into the void, so as to let her wake up slowly.

"Hi," she murmured with a smile and closed her eyes again, snuggling more closely to me and amping up the torture.

Izzy wasn't grouchy in the morning, but she'd always been slow coming around. Especially when we spent much of the night before climbing the mountains of pleasure. And climb we had. We only had a few more days to stuff enough kisses, touches and orgasms in to last us for eight more weeks. Then she'd be back for a spring run. A few weeks after that she'd be back on tour with me as the official band photographer. Then when summer ends we'd figure out how to deal with the last year of my contract with the record label.

I had to figure out how she and I could start our lives officially as an engaged couple.

Once I asked her, that is.

She had no idea I'd bought us a house in LA a few weeks ago. As soon as I saw the listing online, I knew it was perfect for us. Perfect location. Room for both of us to nurture our art and our love. And for months I'd been carrying around a black velvet box in the bottom of my suitcase waiting for the perfect moment to claim her forever.

"I hear your heart beating." Her palm flattened against the flesh over my heart.

"It's saying Isa-belle, Isa-belle." I ran my hand up and down her spine.

"Oh yeah?"

"Yeah. That's all it's ever said. It's a stubborn organ. Only ever learning one tune. The most perfect song in the universe."

She lifted her ear from where it had been tuned in to the rhythm of my life force and grinned at me. "Even when you're being cheesy, your words are so beautiful."

I swatted her butt cheek. "I am *not* cheesy."

She circled her hips and squealed. "Yes, you are. But I love it." Her lips landed on mine. "I love you," the words caressed my mouth before I opened and invited her in.

With a shift of her pelvis and a thrust of mine, two bodies joined much like two hearts already were.

∽

Sweaty and sated, we cuddled, entwined on top of the rumpled sheets. "We should do that again," she panted.

"We can. Later. First, I have a surprise for you."

"Oooo. Is it a one-eyed snake in need of a home?" She managed to keep a straight face while her eyes fluttered innocently.

I guffawed at her and squeezed her tightly to me. The first time she ever saw *it* in the light of day was when we were teenagers. I laughed then at her description, and years later, I still laughed whenever she pulled that line out of her bag of memories. "My one-eyed snake has a home. And after his nap, he'll be happy to slink back where he belongs. While he recuperates, we need to get dressed. I'd rather Joe not see my snake or his cave when he gets here in about fifteen minutes."

That got her moving. She leaped from the bed and threw open her suitcase. "How should I dress?" Clothes were about to be sent into a violent storm of fabric and color.

"Dress comfortably. We'll be walking a bit. And make sure you bring your sketch pad and camera."

She shimmied into a pair of blue jeans and an off the shoulder sweater that somehow matched the pink in her hair perfectly. "This OK?" She didn't bother to look at me while she stuffed her pad, pencils and camera inside a canvas tote.

"Perfect." I continued to watch her. Finally, she met my stare and smirked. "What?"

"Don't you want to get dressed before Joe arrives? Unless he's had to haul your naked self out of somewhere and therefore has seen it all before." She propped her hand on her hip as she contemplated me.

"Nah, he's been spared that. He did have to haul my drunk self out of a few after parties when we first got started. But it's been a while since he's had to hold my hair."

"Your hair isn't long enough to have to hold, crazy boy." She laughed. "Now clothes. On your sexy body. Now." She jabbed her finger in the direction of my clothes.

"I ever tell you how hot you are when you're bossy?" I scooted off the bed and stood with a stretch.

"Quit trying to distract me with your sex appeal. Now that I'm dressed, I want my surprise."

"Yes, ma'am." I saluted her and made a show of shaking my rear as I bent over to grab a pair of jeans. A long-sleeved, gray Henley and a matching gray beanie completed the look. I held out a black beanie to Izzy.

"You think I need a disguise?" Her lip wrinkled in distaste.

"Maybe not. But it might be cold outside. And you *were* sick a couple of weeks ago."

"Ugh. You're right." She slipped the knit fabric over her hair, then moved to check the mirror. "Yeah. It was a rough few days. Almost like the flu, but not quite. But I feel almost as good as new now."

"Yo, D, you guys ready?" Joe shouted from downstairs.

"Just about. Got to grab our coats." I picked hers up from where it was draped over the back of the chair.

"Good. It's like thirty degrees or something out there," Joe informed us.

I held open her long, black coat while she glided her arms inside. Spinning her around, I tugged it up onto her shoulders securely and zipped her up. Digging into her pocket, I pulled out her colorful scarf like a magician. Quickly, I wound it around the slender column of her neck and tucked the tail. From her other pocket, I unearthed her gloves. Like an obedient child, she held out her hand, so I could cover it with the black knitted material. When she held out her bare hand, I took it in mine and placed a kiss on the inked ring around her thumb. Seeing her matching band of commitment never got old. I covered it up with her remaining glove. I loved taking care of her. I couldn't wait to do it on a more consistent basis.

She waited while I donned my leather jacket, scarf and gloves. She grabbed me by my jacket lapels and heated my blood with a branding kiss. Then she zipped my coat up.

We walked down the stairs hand in hand. "You remember when we got our tattoos?" I asked.

"Of course. Let's see." She tapped a finger against her lips like she was pondering. "We were in California for the west coast leg of your first tour. You convinced the label to hire me for the summer to take photos of the band."

"It was our first tour where we weren't the opening act." I thought we were on top of the world back then. Little did I know, it was just the beginning.

"Almost exactly two years ago. We were celebrating our first official anniversary." She squeezed my hand.

"Right. It was a crazy idea. Getting our first pieces of ink together." It was nuts branding our bodies permanently in honor of each other when we were so young. Smiling, I shook my head. Some days we were still those crazy kids, still newly in love, ready to conquer the world using love alone.

We stepped in front of Joe and entered the quiet hallway of the hotel.

"Permanent art symbolizing our unbreakable love." The smile on her face was filled with nostalgia.

"What was the name of the shop again?" My memory for minor details wasn't always great. Too much space occupied by song lyrics.

"Inked Hearts. The artist did a great job creating matching designs that suited each of us yet still looked like they belonged to each other."

"Exactly. I was thinking we should go back and get another one. You could draw us up something else. Our love has grown even more since then. We should commemorate it." I settled her in the cradle of my arms inside the elevator, her back to my front.

"That's a great idea. I'll get to work on it. Any thoughts about what you want?"

"Something musical. It's a badge of honor for rockers. And I'm running behind. How many rock stars have you seen uninked?"

"You have ink."

"Pfft. One small band of ink doesn't count." I tilted my head back and sniffed the air pretentiously.

Joe snickered from his post in front of us.

"I saved the guy's contact info. I'll shoot him an email and start brainstorming ideas."

"Maybe we should use one of the other guys next time... Perhaps the quiet, broody one instead." My fist clenched as I remembered the flirty guy who was way too attentive as he held Izzy's hand so gently while he permanently branded her body.

"What's wrong with the guy who already marked

us? He was nice and talkative. Plus, he did a fabulous job." The confounded look on her face was almost comical.

"He flirted with you too much. I didn't like it."

Her body shook with laughter. "He was just being friendly. Trying to put me at ease," she reasoned as we followed Joe off the elevator and into the parking deck.

"You say potato. I say po-tah-to." I shrugged.

"I didn't notice." She bumped me with her shoulder.

"I did." I pouted.

Joe opened the rear door of the blacked-out SUV we were taking today. As Izzy climbed in, I couldn't resist copping a feel and smacking one rounded cheek.

She yelped in response.

"Couldn't help myself." Everything felt lighter and more playful with her back in my direct orbit.

"Where to?" Joe asked.

"Waffles first at Nicolass's, then on to the surprise."

With a nod, Joe shut us inside and moved around to the driver's side.

"Waffles? Isn't it kind of late for breakfast?"

"You can't come to this part of the world without having waffles. This place has these amazing stroopwaffles. Instead of the thick ones like we have back home, they are these thin waffle layers with a caramel syrup filling in the middle."

A low rumble met my description. "See, your stomach agrees with me. You need waffles."

"It does sound heavenly," she agreed as she snuggled into my side.

"And if you're a good girl, I'll get you an order of *vlaams frites* later on."

"What are those?"

"They're pretty much French fries. But the sauces are ah-mazing." My mouth watered recalling the order I'd had earlier in the week.

"Do they have special bar-b-que sauce or something?" She sounded excited at the prospect

A chuckle erupted. "I'm sure they do. But you have to promise to have a bite of mine. I get mine with their special mayo sauce."

"Mayo on fries? You've got to be kidding me." Her nose wrinkled in disgust.

I bopped her on the nose. "Don't knock it 'til you've tried it."

"Fine. You've never steered me wrong before," she said with a huff.

"And I never will." I winked at her and stole a kiss. "So, how are things going with the studio? You having to resort to posed portraits and event photography yet?" Being an artist wasn't an easy career path. I had full confidence that Izzy would be legendary once her work got in front of the right people. But I always worried that she didn't make enough to take care of herself. Pay her bills, and still pursue her dreams.

"They're going pretty well. Before I left, I had a job photographing the cutest little girl for her third birthday. Her parents wanted no posed shots. Just for me to capture her while she was playing. She was born with a heart defect and wasn't expected to live to her third birthday. So, it truly was a celebration." Her eyes shimmered with emotion.

"That sounds really special. I know her parents will love whatever you did." I stroked her cheek with my gloved finger.

"I hope so. They have lots of friends with kids. If enough people start to recognize the beauty of natural images over posed ones, I'll be able to afford a more permanent studio instead of renting a shared space where I have to work around two other photographers' schedules."

"Is the record label paying you enough for the photography work you do for the band?" I'd stayed out of the negotiations for her pay after I convinced the label to give her a try years ago.

"Yeah. I actually still have some money left from the last batch they bought from me."

I sighed in relief. "Good. I hope you negotiate yourself a pay raise after each gig."

"Don't worry about me. I'm doing fine. My apartment is rent controlled. My blog is making me money through advertisers. Things are good," she assured me.

"I'm so proud of you for chasing after your dreams." I ran my fingers along her jaw.

"I'm so proud of us for not losing *us* during the chase," she whispered. It had been a fear of hers before we ever even took a chance on our love.

Me too. During the band's rise to success we'd encountered many musicians who'd sacrificed love for music. I personally couldn't fathom it. There'd be no music without Izzy. Thankfully the rest of the band fully understood my commitment to her even if the label didn't seem to.

"Yo, D. I almost forgot, Lila said she needed to meet with you later before the show," Joe called over his shoulder as he drove the busy streets.

"Did she say what for? We've already met all our obligations for this week."

"She didn't say. But she seemed to be in a pissy mood." He quirked a brow at me in the rearview mirror.

"What else is new?" I grumbled. The label insisted that Lila handle all of the band's PR work. She was good at her job, but she and I didn't see eye to eye when it came to Izzy or my private life. I was counting the days until I could say goodbye to her interference. Our contract couldn't end soon enough.

"Maybe she wants to talk about the band's sighting in the Red-Light District," Izzy offered.

"Nah. Believe it or not, *that* was good publicity for the band. They were seen out in a rocker appropriate location, and they didn't get out of hand. It was a win for the group. Not something for her to be pissy over."

"Maybe she's not upset." Izzy shrugged and started paying attention to the sights out the windows. Her eyes were bright with wonder, taking in the cacophony of colors lining the canal. "Is that the flower market?"

"Yep. Surprise." She'd always loved flowers, so I couldn't let her come here without the opportunity to capture the beauty of the floating flower market.

A squeal slipped past her lips as she bounced in her

seat. My heart soared with her joy. I lived to put a smile on my girl's face. "Waffles first, though," I cautioned.

Her lower lip jutted out in that way I loved. Leaning toward her, I nibbled her delicate pout until she moaned and granted me admittance. I took everything she offered and gave everything I had.

"Coast is clear, guys," Joe announced as he parked.

"Come on. With the show being tonight, fans will be more vigilant about looking for any of us."

∼

AFTER EATING our fill of heart-shaped waffles, we walked through aisle after aisle of colorful blooms. Izzy snapped pictures at every turn. Every now and then she stopped and sketched things that caught her eye. Watching her turn life into art was inspiring.

People began to glance our way. Conversations were whispered behind cupped hands. A crowd began to grow slowly. They kept their distance, but they were definitely trailing us.

"Time to go." Joe stepped close to us and started herding us to the exit. Clicks and flashes went off behind us. I tucked Izzy's head into my chest and pulled her close as we hurried in the direction of the car.

Once we were safely hidden away from the growing crowd, Joe asked, "Do you want me to drop Izzy back at the hotel, then take you to the venue so you can meet with Lila before the show?"

"No. I'd just as soon she come with us," I answered,

then turned to Izzy. "Unless you need to change or have to go back to the room for something."

"Nope. I'll come get the lay of the land, so I'll be ready to shoot the concert." She snuggled into the cavern under my chin.

"Perfect." I sighed in contentment.

In no time, Joe was parking by the back entrance of the venue. I set Izzy up in my dressing room, then went in search of Lila. It didn't take long to find her. She rounded the corner as I headed toward the green room. The look on her face was not one of happiness. I stopped in front of her and internally braced myself for whatever she was about to go on a tirade about.

"Nice of you to make time to meet with me. I didn't know if you planned to blow off all your responsibilities or not," she remarked snidely. Gripping the fabric on my bicep, she tugged me in the direction of the green room. I snatched my arm away, causing her hand to fall. I didn't need to be led like a petulant child off to time out.

Once we were safely shut inside the green room, I threw myself on the couch, figuring I may as well be comfortable while she ranted about whatever had crawled up her butt. "I'm not sure what's going on. But I know I haven't missed any scheduled appearances or interviews. Remember, I had you schedule everything for *before* Izzy was to arrive, so I'd be free to spend time with her." Lila's attitude had been getting more and more out of hand.

"Yes, you have gone to all the things on the *official* schedule. But you failed to go out with the guys last night, which was a perfect opportunity for the band to gain some more publicity. Instead the guys got noticed, and it's especially noticeable that *you* are absent. That's a problem." She sat next to me.

"Why is that a problem?" My patience was wearing incredibly thin.

"Because what good reason would the front man of a rock band have for skipping out on a night in the Red-Light District with his bandmates?" The look on her face said *how dumb can you be*.

"You know that isn't my scene. Hasn't been for a long time. Neither are the clubs or parties. I tolerate them when I have to. But no way in hell was I going to paint the town in Amsterdam, stirring up false rumors that would only serve to hurt Izzy." I thought my reasoning was pretty sound, and as a woman, Lila should've understood.

"If your girlfriend can't handle the heat of the gossip rags, then perhaps she isn't cut out for a relationship with someone in the spotlight." Her mouth turned down in a frown.

🎼 "Fallen" by Bret Michaels

I ground my teeth. "Izzy is fully aware of the garbage that those tabloids print. And she's certainly capable of ignoring the lies. But I'm not going to provide fuel to a fire that might burn the person I love. It isn't in any of my contracts that I have to be seen out partying and raising hell."

"Fine," she huffed and scooted closer to me. "The label execs aren't happy about the lack of sensational news about you recently, but I'll try to smooth them over. But that brings me to our next issue. Have you seen the latest news about you?"

"No." I shrugged, ready to be done with this conversation so I could get ready for the concert. "You know I don't read articles about me or the band. All that matters to me is the music. I could care less what the latest rumors are about us. They're all stupid anyway—Jett and Brooks are long lost brothers, Maddox is really an alien, Wilder is in love with an alien. Where do they get this crap anyway?"

She didn't even crack a smile at the hilarious headlines I'd just made up. "Well, you'd better start caring. Someone printed photos of you and Izzy strolling hand in hand the other day. Random hookups don't hold hands," she spat.

"We *were* walking down the street, hand in hand as you say. And newsflash, she *is* my girlfriend, not a random hookup. Holding hands is kind of part of it."

She sighed. "A new photo showed up just a little bit ago. The two of you cuddled close."

"Show me the damn photos that have you so bent out of shape." I rolled my eyes as I waited for her to bring up the images on her phone.

She held out her phone to show me. The first article's headline read: *LO front man walks the streets of Amsterdam with... girlfriend?* The photo beneath it was taken at an angle. It showed my profile, but because Izzy was looking up at me, all that could be seen of her was her colorful hair. Our fingers were laced together, and a laugh was on my lips. The photo said more about me than about her. The joy on my face was undeniable.

Lila swiped the screen, bringing up the new article. That headline read: *Rocker, Dawson Anderson cozies up with same girl twice?* The accompanying photo showed me with my arm around Izzy and hers around me. Again, only her hair was visible. But her hair was unique. There was no mistaking that the girl in the photos was the same just wearing different clothes.

"You've never been photographed with the same girl twice. It's noticeable. And *not* in a good way," Lila's voice was carefully controlled.

"I've posed for thousands of photos over the years. *You* make sure the tabloids never show me with the same girl twice when you plant stories for them to print. That's on you. I'm not going to apologize for having a life beyond the band." I was getting so tired of all the crap that went along with being famous. *Wasn't I allowed to have a relationship? Something that mattered to me?*

"Dawson, we've talked about this. You know the label execs agree with me. You officially being in a relationship is bad for the band. Seventy-five percent of the band's album sales are to single girls who all want to dream they have a shot with you. You have to appear single and available. If that's going to be a problem, then maybe the label shouldn't employ Isabelle anymore." Her voice was oddly quiet considering she'd just threatened Izzy's upcoming freelance job.

I drew in a deep breath, then expelled it through my gritted teeth. "Let me make one thing perfectly clear, if Izzy goes, I go. I'll buy out the rest of my contract. Whatever I have to do. The band has been considering its options when our contract is up anyway. Izzy and I have been in a serious relationship for three years now. Not *once* have we ever been photographed inappropriately. This is the first time anyone has even managed to capture an image of us. And you can't even see her face. They don't know who she is. You're making a big deal out of nothing." My fists clenched, and inside I seethed at her nerve.

"It's *my* job to decide what is a big deal. Not yours. And a decline in ticket sales *is* a big deal. Ticket sales dropped on those shows a year ago after it was speculated you were in a relationship. It took me working my magic to negate the effects of those articles. Face it, your bread and butter is horny women who like to think they have a chance of getting in your pants after a show. Best thing you can do is own it for as long as you can. If Izzy really loves you, she'll understand that this is just part of the job. And if she doesn't understand, it's better for you to find out now." There was a hard glint in her eyes.

"Whatever, Lila. We'll be more discreet. We don't have many more outings planned for her trip anyway. We'll be staying in." I got to my feet, trying to send the message that I was done with this conversation.

"And remember, if anyone should approach you or Izzy and asks about a relationship, neither of you are to confirm anything," she warned. "Dawson, you know I have your best interests at heart." She laid her hand on my chest and blinked innocently at me.

"Fine. Now are we done?" I clipped my words.

"For now."

I turned my back and started to leave.

"Dawson," she called from behind me. When I didn't turn around, she continued to speak anyway, "Once Izzy goes back stateside, you should probably make an effort to regain some of your carefree, party attitude from a few years ago. Your contract is up for renegotiation for the upcoming album. You don't want to give the execs a reason to drop your bonuses. Play the manwhore role for a bit. Being photographed with a new groupie on your arm every day will keep the girls coming in more ways than one. And it will make the powers that be happy."

I didn't humor her with anything else. Turning the knob, I purposefully strode into the hallway and went in search of the best anecdote for my boiling blood.

⁓

Hours later, I was still pissed when I left the stage and saw Lila standing next to Izzy. Losing myself in Izzy and then in the music on stage only tamped the rage. Roaring like a freight train, it barreled into my gut. It was time to start counting down the days 'til the end of our contract. Five hundred and forty-four days. *But who was counting?* Besides, we were their cash cow at the moment, so they really didn't want to piss us off. I needed to give the guys a heads up that I mentioned leaving the label to Lila.

They should know I spilled the beans. It wasn't my place to hint at our plans yet.

Forcing a smile to my lips, I greeted Izzy. Something was wrong. I could read her like piece of music. Her eyes didn't sparkle with their usual joy when we entered each other's orbits. Her shoulders were curved in on themselves, shielding her. With calloused fingers, I cupped her cheek and tilted her face up to mine.

"Hey, beautiful. Did you enjoy the show?" My eyes traced every nuance of her face—the worry lines around her eyes, the paleness of her skin, the down tic of the corner of her mouth.

"Mmhmm. I'll never tire of watching you own the stage."

Lila hadn't budged from her spot of wall near Izzy. But I couldn't find a damn to give. So, I did what I wanted, I let my mouth find its home on Izzy's. With a groan of surrender, her lips parted letting me in. It didn't matter that my clothes were sticking to me. Or that I smelled like sweat. Or that people were milling all around us, probably members of the media too. Or that Lila was huffing in anger next to us. Or that my cock was growing painfully hard as it pressed against the cove of her thighs. None of it penetrated our bubble.

A body brushed against my back, jostling us. But it didn't dislodge our lips. If anything, we became more determined in our kiss. In communicating everything we meant to each other. If only I had that black velvet box in my pocket, I'd drop down to one knee and beg for forever. When sparks of light began to flicker behind my eyelids, I knew I had to come up for a real breath of air. Reluctantly, I pulled back and rested my forehead on hers. The sparkle was starting to twinkle in her eyes again. Relief filled me. I'd restore her happiness by the time the night was over.

🎵 "You're All I Need" by White Lion

"Yo, dude. You two going to come hang out with us for at least a little while at the club?" Brooks asked, completely oblivious to the moment he was intruding upon.

A quick look around revealed that Lila was still within earshot. "I'm not so sure that's a good idea," I murmured.

Izzy squeezed my hand. Her touch communicated understanding and acceptance.

"Why not?" Brooks's lips turned down in a frown.

"Because Dawson and I aren't supposed to be photographed together. We're supposed to be *discreet* for the sake of the band," Izzy parroted words that no doubt had been said to her at some point during our show.

"Fuc... I mean screw that," Brooks thundered. "The place we're going is upscale. All celebrities and wannabes. There won't be any cameras there. They don't even let you bring your phones inside."

Leaning back slightly, but still keeping my hands on her hips, I said, "What do you say, flutterby? Want to go dancing with me?"

"I'd love to." My girl loved to dance. And dancing with her was a delicious form of foreplay.

～

Joe parked in a darkened alleyway. As soon as the car doors opened, the air reverberated with a heavy thump. The bass was so loud, it was impossible to discern any hint of the melody.

Ty and Blake led the way to a hidden door and knocked. When it opened a crack, a quick conversation was had before the door was thrown open and we were allowed inside. Joe hovered behind me and Izzy, making sure we were safe in the middle of our pack.

Next to me, Izzy's body started swaying to the rhythm lacing the air. She'd never been able to resist an addictive beat. I paused a few seconds, letting her get a couple of steps ahead of me so I could appreciate the view. The swing of her hips was hypnotic. My fingers twitched, itching to grip her body and move in time with it. She threw a smirk over her shoulder, knowing exactly why I'd slowed down. She tugged my hand forcing me to fall in step with her.

When the front of our group emerged from the long hallway into the large open room, a hostess greeted us. It was impossible to hear the words coming from her mouth, but the accompanying hand gestures let us know space had been reserved for us in a corner of the upper level.

The pulsing crowd parted as we moved toward the staircase in the center of the club. A bar ran along the wall behind us while private booths lined the far wall. To the left was a DJ booth suspended above the masses. Tables were scattered to the right. Most of the available floor space was being utilized for dancing.

There were so many famous faces in the crowd that no one seemed to pay attention to a few more adding to the mix. Some of the tension in my shoulders relaxed with the knowledge that we could just have fun without being "on" for once. We had dressed to blend in, just in case. Plain t-shirts, jeans, ball caps. Izzy had even twisted her hair up into a bun that only allowed the pink to be seen, all the other beautiful hues were hidden within. Lila seemed mollified by it.

When we reached our designated area, a waitress in a skimpy outfit introduced herself to us. Apparently, she would be tending bar in our little corner of the club. I ordered a mint tea and a water. There was no way in hell I planned to let my senses be dulled by anything. Izzy and I were fighting against a ticking clock and every moment was to be savored. Plus, I wanted to make sure I was fully capable of taking care of her while we were out. After the bartender talked up her specialty drink, a Porn Star Martini, Izzy decided to try it.

The young girl quickly got everyone in the group's drink orders and then took her place behind the bar. Efficiently, she began mixing and pouring. We all watched in amazement as she twirled and flipped bottles, creating concoctions like Tom Cruise in *Cocktails*.

Izzy moaned when she took the first sip of her drink, a combination of passionfruit juice and champagne. "The drink's living up to its name already. You're moaning like a porn star after one sip," I teased.

"*I'll* be moaning for you later," she whispered in my ear. Her lips grazed the edge, sending a shiver down my spine.

The track changed. The DJ's smooth voice came over the speakers, "We're going *oude* school now." Then that unmistakable, guttural utterance of "Oh… Oh…" followed by the addictive beat of V.I.C.'s dance song filled the air. Everywhere bodies scrambled to organize themselves into lines.

🎼 "Wobble" by V.I.C.

"Wobble with me," Izzy yelled. She set her glass down on the table and grabbed my hand. We found a spot big enough to accommodate us. We got our wobble on with the rest of the club, but Izzy and I didn't arrange our bodies in a neat line. Rather we moved as a single unit with a miniscule amount of air between us. It was hot as hell, her rear grinding against my crotch as my arms bracketed around her, occasionally anchoring her to me with a palm on her bare abdomen. Back in high school when she taught me this dance, we didn't move together in such a dirty, sensual way. Good thing, my teenaged hormones wouldn't have been able to take it.

One song flowed into another. And another. And another. We bumped and grinded and danced until we were breathless. When a thin sheen of sweat coated our flesh, making us glisten, I asked, "You ready to get out of here?"

"Yes, I'm ready to dance with you in private. Nothing between us but a slow tempo to last all night."

I couldn't drag her to the car fast enough.

Chapter Five
Izzy

My trip to Amsterdam had been a whirlwind of love and lust. But our time together was winding down. I hated it.

Yesterday we slept in after the late night at the dance club. Then we toured the Van Gogh museum. Seeing masterpieces in person that I'd only ever seen in textbooks was inspiring. Dawson bought a reprint of my favorite, "Sunflowers" and arranged for it to be shipped to my apartment. Then we visited Vondel Park and had a picnic. With help from Dawson's stylist, we managed to stay out most of the day without being detected by the press or general public. It was a relief to be able to just be us.

Tomorrow afternoon we had to pack up and drive to Belgium. Thankfully, we had no plans today. No shows, no appearances, no sightseeing, no sharing our time with anyone else.

I stretched blissfully. My muscles tingled with that delicious ache I always got when reuniting with Dawson after a lengthy time apart. Generally, it took us a couple of weeks to get past the ravenous state and settle into a less frantic need for each other. My visit wasn't going to be long enough for us to hit that state, so I'd go home with my muscles still carrying the brand of our intense loving. I smiled at the thought.

Swinging my legs over the edge of the bed, I ran my toes through the plush carpet. I reached for my phone to check the time. After lunchtime. No wonder I was starving. As I set my phone back on the nightstand, my heart soared at the framed photo of me and Dawson that he always put next to his bed no matter where he was. I had the same photo next to my bed. It was one of my favorites. I remembered the day like it was yesterday...

It was early spring, so the weather was nice enough to go to the park, but the air was still brisk. It took me a few tries to find a spot where I could set up my tripod without it sinking in the damp grass. Once I did, I took dozens of shots of Dawson for one of my classes. He was my favorite subject. After much cajoling, he finally convinced me to join him in the frame. With a few setting changes, I arranged for my camera to burst shoot a series of pictures of us.

As soon as I got within reach, Dawson tugged me against him, just as the first shutter click sounded. When he wrapped his hands around my waist and stared into my eyes, the world faded. And so did the camera. By the time we were breathless from kissing, the burst shooting was long over. But the resulting images were stunning. They couldn't have been more perfect if I'd been directing the poses. The passion and love that pulsed between me and Dawson in the frozen frame was a living entity, oozing off the photograph.

Knowing he set that reminder next to his bed no matter where he was, did a lot for easing the doubts which tried to creep into my mind anytime the tabloids decided to target him. With a smile on my face, I stood and snagged Dawson's discarded band shirt. As the soft fabric settled over my skin, I inhaled deeply, breathing him in. Just in case Dawson wasn't alone downstairs, I pulled on a pair of lacey boy shorts from suitcase. The shirt was long enough to conceal all my important parts. Peeking from beneath some of my clothes was a glittery, red package. I shifted my clothes around to unearth Dawson's gift. Snagging my zippered art pouch and the package, I headed for the stairs.

Before I descended, I strained my ears to see if anyone was in the suite besides Dawson. I really didn't want any more run ins with Lila. And I wouldn't put it past her to try to ruin our day in with some unscheduled appearance or another lecture about how I needed to make sure no one knew I was Dawson's girlfriend. *For the sake of his career*. Whatever. That woman just wanted an opportunity to be with Dawson herself. His image had nothing do with her meddling. Hearing only Dawson singing along with the radio, I started down the stairs.

The glass surface of the steps was cold under my bare feet, making me hurry.

When I reached the bottom, I stepped into the open archway of the kitchen. Dawson's back was to me. Clad only in boxers, he was a sight to behold. He was doing something at the counter. His hips shimmied as he danced and sang along with Taylor Swift's "Shake it Off". I stifled a laugh. He'd never let the guys catch him listening to this. They'd give him grief for days. But Dawson had mad respect for Taylor and was a closet fanboy. As he executed a twirl, he noticed me admiring him. Rather than act embarrassed at being caught like most guys would, Dawson owned it. He danced up to me and took me in his arms.

🎵 "Shake It Off" by Taylor Swift

"See something you like?" he teased.

"Very much." I pressed my lips to his neck.

"I was just finishing up and was about to come wake you up." His hips still continued to gyrate.

"You mean after you got your fill of pop music?" No self-respecting rocker would ever own up to listening to pop music for pleasure.

"Exactly." He planted a kiss on the top of my head and moved back to the counter. "You hungry?"

"Famished," I admitted.

"Good. I ordered flatbread pizza from that place the canal guide told us about." He moved toward me with a plate in each hand. The aroma of garlic and tomatoes filled my nostrils as he passed on the way to the table. "Come sit. I'll get the wine," he commanded as he pulled out a chair for me.

I settled at the table we'd yet to use, placing the package and pouch in front of me. The song playing through the speakers switched from pop to rock. Dawson's sensual rasp floated through the air. It was one of my favorites off their last album, "Love Rocked". He moved around the room, a carnal being hypnotizing me with sway of his torso, the thrust of his hips, the seduction of his voice. My gaze stayed locked on him as he worked the room like he did a stage, only this time he performed for an audience of one instead of thousands. Finally, the notes faded, and I was sufficiently hot and bothered.

"Whatcha got there?" he asked as he sank into the chair next to me, wine glasses in hand.

"A gift for you." I tapped the crimson covered box. "And supplies we need for part of your gift." I poked the pouch of art supplies. "You want to open it first?" I slid the box closer to him, knowing he was still very much like a child when it came to presents.

"I'm starving, but you know my weakness." He was torn. His finger toyed with the taped flap on the end of the box. "I have something for you too. Upstairs."

"But you already gave me this trip and the flowers and the Van Gough print," I protested.

"Well, I got you something else. *And* I got something for *us*. Let's eat first. Then we can open the presents."

"You mentioned gifts for me just so I'd be as impatient as you are right now," I admonished, smacking his thigh.

"Hey, fair's fair." He took a healthy bite of pizza.

I followed suit, groaning as the flavors burst on my tongue. It wasn't New York style, but it was really good. We ate in silence. No need to fill it with chatter or noise. The kind of quiet that can only be achieved when two people knew each other inside and out like we did.

After we'd downed two pieces each, Dawson seized the red box. His patience had come to an end. Bits of rose paper littered the tabletop as he shredded the wrapping. Running one calloused fingertip along the taped edge of the box, he finally freed the lid.

"Seriously, flutterby?" he moaned as he took stock of the smaller, wrapped packages within.

I tried to smother my laugh but failed. "Open this one first." I handed him a flat, rectangular package. The thin object flexed in his strong fingers. Once he lifted the paper flaps, he unveiled a small leather-bound journal. "It's handmade. The inserts can be removed, and blank ones added when you fill it up with all the number one hits you've yet to write," I explained.

He unwound the string keeping the covers closed. "Izzy," he gasped as he thumbed through the pages. Scattered throughout the book, I'd doodled on the corners of pages, painted various memories of ours and left little messages to him. "This is perfect. I love it." His fingers reverently rubbed the sketched version of the photo by his bed.

"It should fit in your pocket, so you can keep it with

you for when inspiration strikes."

"I'd see if it fits in my pocket, but that would require putting on pants." His eyes sparkled with mischief.

"Don't even think about it." I nudged the next glossy package toward him. "This one's next."

Picking up the box, he gave it a gentle shake, sending the contents thudding into the edges of the box. *Glad I bubble wrapped them.* With less finesse, he ripped into the foil. Once he'd stripped away the layers of paper, cardboard and cushioning bubble wrap, he palmed two glass jars. Rolling them in his hands, he admired the painting I did on both of them—a dandelion made of music notes, floating off in the wind to become songs. In a fancy script, I wrote on the glass surface "Wishes & Hopes for my Love".

His face was a mask of confusion. "Open the other package, then I'll explain."

Without further question, he made quick work of the last package. His brow furrowed as he fanned out the long, thin strips of colored paper. "Now, I'm really confused."

"So, I know we spend more time apart than either of us would like. And times of distance will probably always be part of our reality for the foreseeable future. So, I thought we could write down hopes and wishes and little messages for each other. Then I'm going to fold them into these cool little wishing stars. And anytime you need to, you can take one out, unfold it and read it."

"Ooookay," his tone was skeptical.

"Let me show you." Grasping the metal tab on my art

pouch, I unzipped it and removed a black sharpie. Quickly, I wrote on a slip of light blue paper. When I finished, I turned it, so he could read my message to him. *I hope you have an epic show.* Then I began folding the ribbon of paper into a pentagon. He watched with rapt attention as I pinched the folded shape. With a couple of presses, the flat shape popped up into an origami star. "A wishing star." I held out the small shape to him. Turning it over and over, he marveled at it.

When he offered it back to me, I dropped it into his jar. I held out my bag of markers to him. After digging through them a moment, he selected a glittery purple one. "Pink might not show up on all the colors well," he offered by way of explanation for his choice. After grabbing a rainbow of colored strips, he shifted in his seat so that I couldn't see what he scrawled on them.

Two could play that game. I got to work writing every wish, hope and message of love I could think of for him.

I wish for you to have sweet dreams.
I hope for our time apart to pass quickly.
I wish for your music to touch more hearts.
I pray Lila stops giving you grief.
I hope you stay positive.
I hope your dreams are filled with me.

All the hopes I held in my heart for him, for us, I poured onto little scraps of paper. I scattered in a bunch of *I love you*'s too. The exercise went much faster than I expected. Soon all the strips carried messages of love. With sure fingers, I showed Dawson how to fold them into pentagons. When he tried to puff the flat shape up into a star, it popped up out of his fingers, flying across the table.

"I'll do the star part," I offered with a giggle.

"That's probably best."

I made quick work of transforming the two-dimensional pieces into three-dimensional stars. By the time I was done, we each had a jar filled with love to help us get through the times when distance made things harder than love should have to be.

"Be right back." He grabbed our jars and dashed up the stairs. While I waited, I carried our dirty dishes to the kitchen. I eyed the bottle of wine. Another glass would taste good. But I didn't want to tip into that sleepy, leaden-limb feeling. That might interfere with our last full day in a room with total privacy. Tomorrow we'd be on a tour bus with several pairs of ears on the other side of the bedroom door.

Strong arms snaked around my waist and tugged me backwards against a muscular chest. Dawson planted a sensual kiss in the sensitive hollow behind my ear. "You know, we never did finish that tour when you got here," he murmured against my skin, sending goosebumps skittering across my skin.

"Really? You want to show me the rest of your suite, now? On our last full day here?" I glanced over my shoulder at him.

"Humor me." He laced his fingers with mine and tugged me through the living room and into a darkened room we hadn't taken the time to explore.

With the turn of a knob beside the entrance, the

recessed can lights warmed and cast a glow around a room with a huge screen occupying one wall. Wide overstuffed chaise lounges were arranged in a couple of loose rows. "Your suite has a-a movie theater?" I stammered.

"Yep. Thought we could watch a movie today. Quiet afternoon in. If that's OK with you."

"It sounds wonderful." Lifting on my toes, I pressed my lips to his.

"But first, open the gift I got for you." He held out a flat pink box to me. "I'll give you the gift I got for us, later."

Carefully, I slid a finger beneath the tape on one end. "Hurry up," he urged. He was always so impatient for me to open my gifts.

With methodical precision, I freed a book from the glittery paper. "Dawson," I breathed as I flipped through the pages of a scrapbook. Photos of us spanning eighteen years adorned the heavyweight pages. Sprinkled amid the pictures were messages, memories, lyrics all written in Dawson's messy scrawl. "How'd you get all these pictures?" Some of them, I hadn't ever seen before.

"I had the help of both our parents, the guys, some of our old classmates and the old yearbook advisor at your school." He ticked off his sources on his fingers.

"How long have you been working on this?" I asked in awe.

"Many months," he muttered. He clasped his hands together behind his back and rocked on his heels. The exact thing he always did when he was nervous.

I couldn't believe how much effort he'd put into an

anniversary gift. "Wow, babe. I love it."

"I thought you could add some drawings to the margins. This can be the book we use to tell our fairytale to our kids one day," he explained.

My heart leaped at his words. "I can't wait to add more pages to our happily ever after."

"Me too, flutterby. A lifetime of love to add to our story," his voice was heavy with emotion.

Clearing my throat, I swallowed down the lump of tears gathering inside. I needed to change the subject, or I was going to bawl over his thoughtfulness. "So, what movie are we watching?" I set the book down on the coffee table and flopped down into one of the lounges.

He moved to the cabinet in the corner to grab the remote and turn on the unit. "Oh, just a little story we're a tad familiar with. And before we start, no complaining about how the book is better than the movie. Let's just go ahead and agree that's the case before we even start, OK?" He waggled his finger at me sternly.

"Agreed."

Dawson turned off the lights as the screen flickered to life. Climbing over the back of the seat, he settled in the lounge with me, tucking me in between his thighs and leaning my back against his front. A sigh of contentment escaped my lips as his arms wrapped around my middle. We'd watched TV in this position countless times over the years. On the screen, clouds moved in fast forward, turning from white to angry grey. As the title of the movie appeared, I turned my head to meet his eyes.

"We're watching *Fifty Shades*?" My insides heated

with the possibilities.

"Yeah. We enjoyed reading the books together and discussing the chapters in our daily video chats. I thought it would be fun to watch the movie sharing the same space." His smile was uncertain, like he thought I would protest watching it with him.

"Sounds good," my voice had a rough edge to it. Reading scenes from the books together had led to some of our hottest video chats. I couldn't fathom what infernos would arise from watching the movie practically in his lap. But I was more than willing to fan the flames.

Throughout the movie, Dawson kissed and caressed me here and there, stoking the fire building within me, but never letting it engulf me. Whenever I got close to the edge, the scene would end, and his lips would leave my heated flesh and his fingers would settle back into the neutral territory of my abdomen. It was frustrating. But glorious. From the hard ridge at the small of my back, I wasn't alone in my feelings.

🎼 "Love Me Like You Do" by Elle Goulding

By the time the movie ended, I was a needy mess. The finality and sadness of the last scene didn't dampen the blaze Dawson had been building for the past couple of hours. His tight hold around my middle didn't allow me to shift or turn toward him. He was hard against my back, and I couldn't do anything to get things moving in the direction I was desperate for.

"So, what did you think about the movie? As good as

the book?" he murmured in my ear.

"You really want to discuss the differences between the book and the movie right now? With your cock trying to press a hole in my back in a blind attempt to get where it belongs? With me practically dripping on this expensively upholstered chair?"

With one arm still keeping me firmly anchored in place, he snaked his other hand lower, barely brushing where I yearned for him to touch. "Yeah, I want to talk about the movie while it's fresh in our minds. Speaking of minds, it was kind of nice not being in *her* head so much. I wondered how all that inner dialogue would translate to the movie."

His fingers stroked the fabric covering me infinitesimally harder. "Uh... yeah," I stuttered.

"And I was so glad they left out the tampon scene. Not saying it wasn't hot. But I don't think it would've been hot on screen." He nuzzled the soft spot behind my ear. "Izzy, did you think the movie was hot?"

Dawson's touch became quicker. Harder. "Mmh-mm," I moaned and tried to wiggle into his caress, but his firm hold didn't allow it.

He pressed hot, sucking kisses to my neck. His ministrations continued below my waist. "I thought it was hot. Watching it with your body against mine. Remembering reading some of the scenes out loud with each other during our video chats. Running my fingers and lips over your skin while you stared at the screen. Bringing you pleasure, *only* pleasure, never pain. It was all hot as hell. Now... don't come." He tweaked my nub gently through my drenched panties before removing his hands from my body. "Yet." Gripping my chin, he turned my face more fully to his, so he could plunder my mouth.

When we read the elevator scene in the book, we talked about Christian telling her to not give into the pleasure he rained on her body in a crowded elevator. And how the command to not to come was ridiculous. We actually both laughed about it.

I wasn't laughing now. Pleasure thundered in my veins, trying to wash over every nerve ending. Demanding I yield. With an effort I didn't know I possessed, I managed to rein it in. Barely.

I was breathless when our mouths disconnected. With strong hands, he shifted our bodies to the edge of the seat. He set me on trembling legs and led me up the stairs.

My weak knees barely carried me to our room. Just before I collapsed on the bed in a "take me now" position, Dawson tugged me back. Sure fingers divested me of the little bit of fabric adorning my body. Then he stripped out of his boxers. Hot hands planted on my hips and turned me to face him fully. "You want to play a little more first?"

Such a tough decision. More play meant delayed gratification. But I was already an exhibit in delayed gratification. But... past experience told me that it'd be well worth the torturous wait. Swallowing the excitement clogging my throat, I drew in a deep breath. "A little. But I don't think I can take a lot more," my voice was breathy.

"The movie inspired me a little." Mischief twinkled

in his eyes as worry swirled in my guts. Pain was not anywhere on my radar of want. My threshold for it was miniscule. I was all about pleasure. Dawson usually was too.

"Inspired you how?" I whispered, my voice hoarse.

"We happen to be in like the sex capital of the world or something. So... I might have picked up a few things in anticipation of your visit. But you have nothing to worry about. I'd never hurt you. The thought of you in pain makes me sick to my stomach. I didn't buy any floggers or paddles," he joked.

"Or clamps?" The thought of metal teeth pinching my sensitive skin terrified me.

"Or clamps. Trust me?"

"Always." I gave him a weak smile.

"Then get on the bed," his command was gruff, laced with need.

I spun toward the bed. He swatted one cheek as he moved to his suitcase.

"Hey! You said no pain," I teased.

"Couldn't resist. But seriously, no pain. I promise." He held up his hand in a scout's honor pose.

With quick hands, I folded down the blankets. Then I lay back on the soft pillows, anticipation keeping me from sighing in contentment at the comfort of the cloud beneath me. I watched as Dawson withdrew something from his bag, but I couldn't tell what it was. A small zippered bag dangled from his fingertips as he made his way to where I waited. He sank down on the mattress next to me. The hiss of the zipper was ominous in a room where the only audible sounds were our breaths. Leaning forward, I tried to peek into the dark recesses of the bag.

"Un-uh. No peeking." He rifled through it and unearthed a dark blindfold and a length of red ribbon.

"Is that from Paris?" I asked, recognizing the expanse of silky ribbon I'd wrapped myself in this past Christmas when I visited him on tour.

Shrugging, he grinned at me. "I thought it might come in handy one day. Can I use it to tie your hands to the bedframe?" He wound it around his fingers while he waited for me to answer.

Heat flared. The thought of being bound—unable to move, to stop him, to touch him—was scary. But it was incredibly arousing too. I chewed my lower lip as I contemplated my options.

"If you don't want to, it's OK. And if we try it and you don't like it, just tell me, and I'll untie you," he offered. He looked at me bashfully.

"OK," I breathed out.

Dawson drew me to him and kissed me deeply, erasing any lingering fear and anxiety. When our mouths separated, his forehead rested on mine. "You sure you're OK with this?" He held up his hand with the ribbon intertwined between his fingers.

"I'm sure," I whispered.

He rearranged the pillows before easing me back into their fluffy embrace. Taking one of my hands in his, he brought it to his mouth and pressed a kiss to my palm. Gently, he wrapped my fingers around one of the gilded spindles adorning the headboard of the bed. Deftly he wrapped the scarlet strip of satin around my wrist, anchoring it loosely to the metal. His lips trailed from my wrist, down my forearm, up to my shoulder. Goosebumps rose in the wake of his kisses. With tenderness on his face and in his touch, he grasped my other hand and repeated the process of looping the ribbon lightly around my wrist and the headboard.

"You good?" he asked as he ran his fingers in between the binding and my skin.

"Yeah," I breathed out, tugging gently against the ribbon. "Do I need a safe word?" I was only halfway teasing.

"*Stop* works for me." He winked.

I swallowed hard and nodded. Soft fingers brushed the strands of hair from my forehead, tucking them behind my ears. He slipped the blindfold over my eyes, casting the room into utter darkness. Panic rose as my sight diminished, until a calming touch traced my cheek.

"Shh. You're OK," Dawson murmured against my lips. Instantly, the worry receded.

He drew my lower lip between both of his and nibbled. His tongue slipped into my mouth to tangle with mine. My hands flexed and pulled against my bindings with the need to touch him. He pulled back, his mouth barely touching mine. My head lifted, straining to maintain contact with him. When his mouth was free of mine, I couldn't stop the cry that slipped out over the loss of physical connection. In the dark, all my other senses trained on him. The scent of his spicy, sweet cologne. The soft pants of his breath. The heat of his body hovering over mine. The taste of him still lingering on my lips.

He dropped kisses along my skin sporadically at random spots. I tried to anticipate where his lips or fingers would land, but there was no rhyme or reason I could decipher to his movements. The shifting of his weight on the mattress further threw off my ability to guess where I'd be touched next. A kiss on my collarbone. A calloused finger dragged along my ribs. A nibble under the swell of my breast. A light scratch down my inner thigh. A tickle to my knee. A bite to my earlobe. A kiss to the arch of my foot.

The longer I lay in the dark, bound not only by satin but by desire as well, the more sensitized I became. Each touch twisted me more tightly on the inside. Spots on my body that had never been erogenous zones suddenly were hardwired to my core.

My heart knocked against my ribcage like a trapped bird trying to fly free. My breath stuttered in and out of my chest as my body climbed the hill of a roller coaster. Being robbed of my sight meant I had no idea how tall the climb was going to be before I crested and zipped down the other side.

I was dying and flying inside.

Dawson shifted down on the bed. His touch disappeared from my body. It was an aching loss. I whimpered in impatience. His chuckle sounded somewhere halfway down the mattress. "You still doing OK, flutterby?" his voice was gruff.

"Yep." The unaffected tone I was shooting for fell

hilariously short. My voice was just as needy as his.

Strong hands gripped my thighs and pushed them further apart. *Finally, he was about to be where I wanted him. Where I needed him.*

The mattress dipped as he got into position. His thumb slid between my folds. The cool metal of his thumb ring created a glorious friction. "You're drenched, baby."

"I know. I need…" I couldn't finish. I needed so much. One thing, a thousand things. Something. I was almost to the point of shamelessly begging.

One finger dipped inside. Barely. I writhed in frustration. If my hands were free, I'd direct him to touch me where I needed him. Being at his mercy was a head rush and an exercise in a patience that I'd never possessed when it came to him.

He gave a tiny twist and stroke. It relieved the ache for an instant. But it wasn't enough.

Then it disappeared. The bed shifted again as he moved.

I couldn't figure out what he was doing. All my senses strained to decipher the situation, to paint the picture in my mind. Coarse hair tickled the sensitive flesh of my thighs. A finger circled my belly button. Any other time, and the feather light touch would have made me giggle. Not today.

His hard tip strained against my center. I sucked in a sharp breath as it stroked my sensitive flesh, brushing against my concentrated bundle of nerves. His cock slid lower and eased inside. He gave me a short, teasing stroke. It left me yearning for more. My inner muscles clenched around his fleshy length, trying to draw him in deeper or at least prevent his escape. After a handful of strokes, each one getting infinitesimally longer, he was finally stroking that magic spot inside my body. He was a perfect fit and the perfect angle, like we were created for each other. My knees bent, and my feet scrabbled to give me leverage. My hips needed to thrust up into his movements. To meet him.

Before I could get my feet flat and stabilized, a gentle flicker brushed my clit. It felt amazing. But different. Not like his normal touches when we made love. I forced myself to concentrate on the difference. The pressure was different, less. The touch was more... dexterous somehow. Heat caressed my damp flesh. Moisture increased. Another full stroke into my body scattered my thoughts.

I recognized the feeling, the touch... and the strokes. But normally the two weren't in conjunction with each other. Because it was impossible for Dawson to be buried inside of me and still licking my intimate folds. The realization froze my heart.

He wouldn't.

Fear stole some of my pleasure. We'd never talked about adding anyone to our lovemaking before. I was open-minded about a lot of things. But not that. Never that. I didn't share well.

My wrists twisted and turned as I tried to free myself. "Stop," I choked out as tears spilled from my blind eyes.

"OK. It's OK, flutterby." His weight disappeared

from my lower half as he hastily shifted to the head of the bed. Gentle fingers lifted the material from my eyes. Though the light in the room wasn't bright, I still had to blink a few times against the sudden light. Dawson worked to free my hands while I glanced around the room, looking for another person. But I saw no one.

He rubbed the irritated skin of my wrists where I'd pulled against the ribbons. Once he was satisfied that my circulation was good, he turned his attention to my tear stained face. "Baby, what's wrong? Did the ribbon hurt you?" He tugged me into his embrace, pressing my head to his muscled chest.

"Where is he?" my voice trembled as I asked.

"He?" Dawson leaned back to look in my eyes. "Who are you talking about, baby?"

"The other person who was in here. The one who was lic-licking me." My breathing was erratic, fear still gripping me.

"Flutterby, there's nobody here but us. I swear." His voice was so earnest. I wanted to believe him.

"But how? You can't do both those... things at the same time. You're good, but you're not that good."

"Vibrator."

"No way. That felt real. It felt like... you." I'd tried several toys over the years with Dawson. None felt like real flesh. And the size and angle were *his*. I just knew it.

"It's part of the gift I got for us. Let me show you." He fumbled for something midway down the bed. Opening his palm, he revealed a hot pink vibrator. I frowned. It couldn't have been...

"Go on take it," he urged.

Gingerly, I plucked it from his grasp. The weight and texture of it felt real. Dawson shuffled to his feet and moved to his suitcase. I ran a fingertip over the texture of my new toy. The bumps and veins were familiar, in a way a toy shouldn't be. For years I'd been intimately acquainted with every part of Dawson's anatomy. The appendage I held in my hand was a *really* good replica. It was impossible. In disbelief, I leaned back against the pillows.

Dawson sank down next to me, his hands filled with something else and our phones.

"How?" astonishment coloring that single word.

"Told you, sex capital of the world. You'd be surprised what's available for a price." He smirked at me.

"I can imagine. But how did you find a toy so close to you know... *you*?" *Why was I so embarrassed discussing this?*

"I used a mold," he explained matter-of-factly.

"*What?* That's a thing?"

"Apparently. Go ahead, compare. I know you want to." He gestured between his body and the imitation I held in my sweaty palm.

He knew me so well. Reaching over, I traced a fingertip over his sensitive foreskin. He drew in a sharp intake of breath. The vein ridges were in the same place on the toy. I gave him a few test strokes, making his breath hiss back out. The shape and size of the two were a match. A perfect likeness.

"Wow."

"Being a duplicate isn't all that is." Dawson swiped across his phone screen and with a few taps, the object in my hand began to vibrate.

Startled, I squealed and dropped it. Dawson guffawed at me. With delicate fingers, I picked it up again. "What did you do?"

"That is a long-distance toy. It's blue-toothed enabled. So, I can control the vibrations with an app on my phone no matter where I am in the world. It also has a button on it like a normal vibrator, so you can work it too."

"You mean that when we're apart, you can... and I can..." I still couldn't comprehend the possibility.

"Yeah. It's part of a duet," he informed me.

"Huh?"

He opened a box and pulled out a sheath. "This is the part I keep, and you control it with your phone."

I took the device from him and rubbed my fingers inside. Subtle bumps and ridges lined it.

"So, we can use these to play with each other when we're oceans apart?" *How was it possible?*

"That's the idea." He winked at me.

"Definitely something to look forward to when I get back stateside then." I grinned at him shyly.

"Happy anniversary, flutterby. I love you," he declared and kissed my mouth quickly.

"I love you too."

He took our new toys from my hands and placed them on the nightstand. "Now, how about we finish what I started a little bit ago?"

Chapter Six
Dawson

🎼 "Heaven" by Kane Brown

After a leisurely morning of enjoying the comforts of a large, non-moving space, it was finally time to board the bus again. But loving on a bus was something Izzy and I had perfected over the years. We had a couple more days before we had to say goodbye again. And we'd spend those days in motion. Literally.

"You have all your stuff?" I asked as I took one more look around the bedroom.

"I think so." She was walking through the room, double checking everywhere. Bending over, she swooped up a stray pencil from the floor and tucked it back into her art pouch.

Joe had some of the guys stop by yesterday to move Izzy's flowers and some of our other belongings to the bus. We each only had a suitcase left. I zipped them shut and carried them to the head of the stairs.

"I'm going to miss this place," Izzy said, spinning around to take in the room one more time.

"Why?" I'd had the same thought myself, but I didn't understand why. Izzy and I had spent time together all over the world. "What makes this place different for you than all the other hotels we've stayed?"

Her brow crinkled as she looked into my face. "I'm not really sure. Just a feeling. I can't really explain it. It's just more special somehow. More significant."

"I agree. But I don't understand why either. Just something in my gut or maybe my heart. But I'll make you a promise. We'll come back here for our fifth anniversary and any other time you want to come that we can make it work. Deal?"

"Deal. Maybe we can come for our honeymoon one day." Her confidence in our future was everything to me. The smile on her face lit my whole world. I hoped my answering one did the same for her.

"Come on. Time to roll out." I hoisted up our suitcases and led the way down the stairs. As we reached the bottom, a knock vibrated the door.

"Right on time," I announced as I opened the door to Joe's serious face.

"Ready to go, guys?" He was in no nonsense mode today. He always was whenever the band was on the move. It was when we were the most vulnerable.

"Yep," I answered.

"Good afternoon, Joe," Izzy said, greeting him with a

kiss to the cheek, refusing to allow his gruffness to linger.

His stern expression cracked into a grin for her. "It *is* a good afternoon, Izzy." Taking the bags from me, Joe handed them off to one of the guys in the hallway. "Everyone's already loaded out except you guys. We're actually ahead of schedule for a change. So, if you're not quite ready, we have some time to spare."

"We're good. Might as well get this show on the road," I said, lacing Izzy's fingers with mine and filing out of our haven.

∽

After a short drive across town, we pulled into the lot where the buses were waiting. The road crew milled around the buses, triple checking to make sure all of our gear was safely stowed. Joe parked next to the band's bus. When the back door opened, sunlight flooded in. I scrambled out then helped Izzy.

As we boarded the bus, the chaos of cramming five rowdy musicians into a finite amount of space greeted us.

"Izzy," the guys shouted in unison as her head broke the top of the stairs.

"Hey guys." She laughed as she was swept up into a line of hugs which passed her further into the interior of the bus. They tugged her down onto one of the couches and started bombarding her with conversation.

"Hey to you too," I mumbled when no one greeted me.

"We see you all the time, dude. We don't get much

time with our girl here," Wilder proclaimed.

"*My* girl. She's my girl," I protested gruffly even as I winked at Izzy.

"Semantics," Jett said as he leaned forward to capture her attention.

"You've got five minutes. When I get back down from putting our suitcases upstairs, I expect space to sit with *my* girl."

Grumbles followed me as I moved through the living area and kitchen on my way to the stairs next to our jam room at the back of the bus. My steps echoed in the small space surrounding the handful of stairs leading to the upper level of the bus.

My nostrils filled with lemony freshness. The clean smell wouldn't last long. This leg of the tour was non-stop shows and appearances. That meant no hotel stays, so no time for a cleaning service to come in and scrub away the stench that only a group of guys in close quarters could accumulate. The sliding doors to each bunk were open, showing the guys had stashed their stuff already. The junk bunks had various bags stashed in them already too. I couldn't remember whose turn it was for the bedroom up front, but the back bedroom was mine. It had been mine from the beginning of this tour. Perk of being the lead singer and throwing in the extra money to buy the bus.

I'd done my stint in the bunks when we first started out. It stifled my creativity. So, when we had the opportunity to purchase this bus from another band, we jumped on it. Two bedrooms and six bunks—it was perfect for a group of five musicians. Well as perfect as a tour bus could be. I dumped our suitcases on the bed and headed back to the lower level.

Back in the living room, I shoved Wilder out of the way, so I could sink onto the couch next to Izzy. Everyone vied for her attention. I was willing to share for a little while. She ate it up. She'd known the guys from the beginning. They each held a special place in her heart. They had no idea how she worried and fretted over them. But they loved her too. I'd seen bands deal with drama because of one of the members' significant others. I was blessed that Izzy wasn't a problem for the guys. And that they respected my relationship enough not to give me grief for skipping out on all the after-party festivities.

"What did I miss?" I settled Izzy's legs over my lap.

"I was asking the guys what they wanted me to cook for them while I'm on the bus for the next few days," Izzy answered, filling me in.

"Let me guess." I tapped my finger against my chin in mock contemplation. "You guys want lasagna." They were so predictable.

"You know it," Brooks cheered. "Nobody makes lasagna like Izzy does."

"Well, technically, my mom makes lasagna like me since it's her recipe. But I'll take the compliment," Izzy answered with a smirk.

Her mom's recipe was to die for.

"We watching a movie or shooting shi—I mean crap?" Jett asked, casting a sheepish look at Izzy as he held up a gaming controller.

It never ceased to amaze me how Izzy's presence always eradicated the crude language from the guys' vocabulary. It had nothing to do with her being a girl. It was their respect for her. Their treatment of her warmed my heart. I'd hate to ever have to choose between Izzy and the band.

"Can we watch *The Notebook*?" Izzy asked.

"Hell no," Maddox shouted from the other sofa.

"Why not? You got something against a classic love story?" Jett challenged him. He would never choose to watch the sappy love story on his own. But he was always trying to be Izzy's favorite.

"I've got nothing against a love story. Especially love getting a second chance. But come on, do you all really want to be reminded that most of us aren't so lucky?" Maddox looked at each of us with his eyebrow quirked.

"It's not like that. It should give you hope for the future," Jett said.

"Besides, is that really what you want right now? Forever love? I mean you get all the pus—I mean... *girls* you want. You ready to give that up?" Wilder asked.

"Life *is* good right now. And I *do* enjoy the fruits of our labor. I didn't mean to open a philosophical discussion on love with my comment," Maddox grumbled.

"We don't have to watch *The Notebook*. We can watch *Mission Impossible* Twenty or whatever if you guys want," Izzy offered, ever the peacemaker.

"We can watch action movies anytime. You're only here for a few days. And *The Notebook* is a good movie.

We can watch it," Maddox conceded, ready to put a smile back on Izzy's face.

She clapped her hands and bounced in her seat.

"I'll pop the popcorn," Brooks said, moving into the kitchen as the bus rumbled to life beneath us.

Everyone shifted around to their preferred seats for watching TV. I moved to the corner of the couch and dragged Izzy between my thighs. When she melted back against me, I ran my nose along the smooth column of her neck.

"No funny business during the movie, mister," she murmured to me, squeezing my thigh.

"Yes, ma'am." I chuckled against her skin. I'd never start anything in front of the guys. Years ago, when I was single, I didn't have a filter. I did what I wanted and didn't care who watched or participated. All that changed with Izzy though. "I'll behave. I promise."

∼

As the movie ended, Izzy swiped her fingers across her eyes. "Every damn time," she muttered, flicking away the tears gathered along her lower lashes.

"I think it's sweet that you cry over sappy love stories," Maddox said.

"Not *every* love story. But I've always been a sucker for a second chance romance. I think it's so sweet how their love lasted through time and distance and others until they were able to find each other again. And once they reunited, nothing could part them, not even death."

"It's grand and all. But you know who I feel sorry for? Lon. He got the shaft. He loved Allie too. And he was a good guy. But he lost at love," Wilder stated, ever the cynic.

"Yeah, that was sad," I agreed. "But he was never supposed to get the girl. Allie and Noah are forever."

A glance at the time told me we still probably had about forty-five minutes before we arrived at the venue. Before we could further discuss the winners and losers in the love story, all our phones vibrated with a text message simultaneously. Jett did the honors of reading it, "Steve says we have not quite three hours before sound check. We have a radio interview as soon as we get off stage. Then we're pulling out as soon as that's done to make it Luxembourg for an appearance in the morning."

"Well, it was nice having a few days of down time. Guess it's back to the grind now," Brooks groaned, getting to his feet. "I'm going to take a nap. Wake me for sound check."

"Since we'll have a late night tonight, I think it's time to get settled into our room," I said, setting Izzy on her feet.

"You mean *your* room," she corrected. She stretched her muscles, then tucked her hands into the back pockets of her jeans.

I gripped her elbow, tugging her to me. "Even when you aren't here, your presence is the *only* thing that makes it feel like home. So, it's our room."

"Awww. You guys are so sickly sweet," Wilder teased while fake gagging.

"This sickly-sweet girl was going to cook you breakfast in the morning. Maybe I shouldn't be so sweet," Izzy taunted.

"He takes it back. Say you take it back," Jett demanded, putting Wilder in a headlock and messing up his perfect hair.

"Fine, fine. I take it back." Wilder laughed.

"I'll make a grocery list, so Jimmy can swing by to get the ingredients for a good breakfast for you boys," Izzy offered over her shoulder as she headed to the stairs.

When we were safely behind the bedroom door, I pressed her back to the door and kissed her like the world was ending. "As much as I'd love to continue this and lose myself in you, we should probably rest. It's going to be a long night," I murmured against her lips.

"We've got tonight. So, I think I could go for a nap right now. But first I need to take care of something."

🎼 "Without You" by My Darkest Days

Izzy set about unpacking my suitcase, turning the room back into my home away from home. I toed off my shoes and slipped out of my jeans while she put away my clothes and toiletries. Once she plugged in my phone charger and returned the framed photo of us to its usual spot by my bed, she turned to me.

"Where do you want this?" she held out the beautiful drawing she was working on a few days ago.

"You finished it?" I hadn't seen her work on it anymore.

"Yeah, while you were sleeping the other night." She shrugged. "If you changed your mind and don't want it anymore, that's OK."

"Of course, I want it. I'd love to frame it and hang it up in here. But I don't want the guys to see it and start picturing you naked." The possibility made my blood start to boil a little.

"Yeah, that would be weird." She scrunched up her nose, considering the possibility.

"One day, we'll frame it and hang it up in our bedroom. And when you're mad at me for leaving the seat up or my socks on the floor or drinking from the milk carton or teaching our son a cuss word, I'll direct you to look at your creation inspired by how much we love each other." I held my hands out to my side and shrugged my shoulders in an innocent gesture.

She laughed. "And in the meantime?"

"Ummm. Put it in the nightstand drawer. That's where I keep the scrapbooks you've made me and our memory box." It would be safe in there.

The drawer whispered open. She pulled out the largest of the scrapbooks and gently placed the thick paper inside, taking great efforts to lay it flat so it wouldn't be damaged. Quietly, she pushed the drawer back in, tucking our precious mementos away for safe keeping.

Satisfied that my room was set up, she slipped out of her jeans. I tugged my shirt off, then pulled down the sheets. I settled into the soft mattress and drew Izzy down with me. With her tucked in my arms, we both drifted off to sleep.

🎼 "You and Me" by Lifehouse

THE DAYS PASSED TOO QUICKLY. Long before I was ready, it was time to bid Izzy goodbye. I skipped out on an interview, so I could see her off. Lila sent me half a dozen angry text messages on the ride to the airport, all of which I ignored. The entire drive I clutched Izzy to me as if I'd never see her again.

"Goodbyes suck," she pouted with her head tucked against my heart.

"Yeah, they do. You should have Wi-Fi on the plane, so we can chat tonight. You'll be home tomorrow, and we'll video chat." I tipped her head back, so I could look into her emerald eyes. I waggled my brows at her as I said, "And we can try out our new toys."

A blush crept over her skin, and her gaze filled with need. "It won't be the same."

"I know, baby. But you'll be back in a couple of months. And then once summer gets here, we won't have to go through these long separations again. We'll get through it." I was determined to at least *look* strong for her. But honestly, each time we had to say goodbye sucked more than the previous time. The length of our separation didn't matter. It was the fact that we'd been enduring separations our whole relationship. We were both tired of it.

"Sorry, I'm being such a downer. I know you need to be getting into your performance mindset."

"You don't have anything to apologize for. Not a damn thing. Soon, this will be different. When the band is the one calling the shots, I promise things will be different," I vowed.

The car slowed to a stop as Joe parked along the front curb at the airport. "Did you remember everything?" I asked still holding her tightly against me.

"I think so. If I forgot anything, you'll just have to keep it until I get back. And if it's something critical, I'll just have to come back sooner, or you'll have to deliver it to me."

"Sounds like a plan." I chuckled.

The backdoor opened, letting in the swish of tires on wet pavement, a random car horn blaring in the distance, the chatter of people bustling about. But none of the noise drowned out the sound of my heart cracking with the weight of another goodbye.

I eased her out of my embrace, so I could exit the car. Before I got out, I tugged my beanie down low on my head, so I could try to blend in. Joe stood at the rear of the car with Izzy's suitcase in hand. She clasped the hand I offered her and climbed from the warm interior into the chilly, wet air. Standing in front of me, the wind blowing through her rainbow-colored hair, she was a vision of sunshine in a world of grey thunderclouds. She had no idea how beautiful she was. Or how she lit up my world. She always had.

Her arms wrapped around my middle, squeezing me tightly and holding all my important parts in. My heart and soul longed to leave with her. "You don't have to come in with me. You don't know what the crowd will be like in there," she offered in a brave voice that only wobbled at the end.

"There's no way I am missing one second with you. I have my disguise." I winked and tugged the edge of my beanie.

Relief filled her eyes that *this* moment wasn't goodbye. Not yet. Winding one arm around her waist, I drew her securely to my side. I walked her slowly into the airport, like a condemned man on the way to the gallows.

Hmm... maybe there was a song in this. Goodbyes like a noose. Farewells like bullets from a firing squad. Shaking my head, I filed the lyrics away for later.

With our hands tucked in each other's back pockets and Joe trailing close behind, we made our way into the bustling lobby of the airport. People swarmed around us like ants marching. Nobody even glanced our way. When we reached the security gate, no amount of sweet talking to the head of security could get me beyond the metal detectors. He did at least let us hang out nearby, so we could have a private farewell.

Perched on a bench in a forgotten corner, we snuggled, quietly absorbing as much of the other as we could. My cells strained to consume her essence through osmosis.

Her fingers played with the neckline of my shirt. "Oh, I forgot to tell you, I loaded a few series of books on your kindle for us to read together."

"That's great. What did you get for us?" I sifted the long, colorful strands of her hair between my fingers, memorizing the feel of it as I inhaled the scent of her shampoo.

"Ummm. *Filthy Beautiful Lies* by Kendall Ryan and the follow up book to it. It's about a girl who auctions off her virginity to save her sister. It's supposed to be hot. Then there was a series by Cassia Leo called the Shattered Hearts series. It's about a couple who falls in love when they're teenagers. And the guy winds up becoming a rock star. They go through some obstacles. When I read the blurb, I thought it would be fun for us to read. There are a few others I put on there. We can figure out which one to read first later."

I captured her hand that was tracing a line along my collarbone. I brought the tips of her fingers to my lips, pressing a kiss to them and then flattening her palm against my beating heart.

I crooned softly in her ear, "If I could, then I would—"

🎼 "Wherever You Will Go" by The Calling

"Don't," she murmured back. "I'm barely holding it together. If you finish that song right now, I'm going to lose it."

In my heart, I finished serenading her with the words that had hurt and healed both our hearts so many times over the years. She snuggled closer to me, like she knew what was on repeat in my head. We just held each other until the last possible moment. The security guard cleared his throat. When we turned in his direction, he tapped the face of his watch to remind us of the time. "I'd better go," she whispered in a shaky voice, fisting the fabric of my shirt in her fingers.

Her jade orbs transformed into shimmery pools. I blinked hard, trying to hold back my own tidal wave of sadness. My thumb rubbed the soft skin beneath one eye, catching a lone tear before it had a chance to mar her gorgeous face. I cradled her cheek and pressed my mouth to hers. The world faded into nothing, narrowing to her skin against my palm, her breath fanning my cheek, her strawberry scent filling my nostrils, her lips on mine, the salt of her tears flavoring our kiss. Just she and I. Two hearts, one beat.

"I love you, flutterby," my voice was thick with the emotion I was holding back. My hard swallow was like a dam made of popsicle sticks trying to contain a tidal wave.

"I love you too, baby," her declaration tattooed my lips. She gave me one more hard squeeze and the briefest of kisses before she grabbed her bag from Joe and speed walked through security. I watched as she was swallowed up by the sea of passengers all flying off to parts unknown.

When she was almost out of sight, she turned and gave me a sad smile. I blew her a kiss and waved goodbye. And the countdown began. Sixty-four days before she'd be in my arms again.

Chapter Seven
Izzy

Shoving the door open, I dropped my suitcase just inside my apartment and wrestled my keys from the lock. Twenty-four hours of traveling was exhausting. Adding the pain of missing Dawson to that, and I was ready to collapse in my bed. I flipped the light switch and gasped. Perched in the middle of my coffee table was a vase of kaleidoscope roses. New roses. Fresh roses. I hadn't been able to bring my others with me, so I left them all over Dawson's room and the bus. Though I longed to flop down and wallow in self-pity over what the coming months would be like without my heart, I beamed as I plucked the card from among the rainbow blooms.

Thought you needed some extra love and color at home to help you get through the next few weeks. I love you, flutterby. ~Daw

Shaking my head, I smiled through my tears. *How did he always know exactly what I needed even when I didn't know?*

A vibration came from my pocket. Fishing my phone out, I grinned at Dawson's timing. With a swipe, his face filled my screen.

"Hey, flutterby. You're home." It was a statement, not a question since he could see my living room behind me.

🎵 "Miss You Like Crazy" by Natalie Cole

"Yeah, baby. Just got in a few minutes ago. There was a delay on the last leg of my flight. Bad storm along the coast."

"I saw that when I checked in on your flight. It's not snowing at home is it?"

"No snow here. The storm is further north. It's a little too warm for more than a cold rain here."

"That's good. You don't need to be out in snowy weather since you were sick not that long ago."

"Yeah." My sudden and intense bout with a virus a few weeks ago really worried Dawson. He hated that no one was here to take care of me.

"How was your flight after we stopped chatting?"

"Pretty good. I worked on an idea for our next tattoos. Wanna see?"

"Of course," his voice was eager.

I grabbed my sketchbook from my tote bag and flipped to the pages. I turned the screen to show him a tribal guitar wrapped with lines of sheet music. Notes dotted the coiling staff.

Dawson began humming the notes. "Is that 'Wherever You Will Go', a part of the chorus?"

"Yeah. And here's what I drew for me." I flipped the page and showed him an elegant flowing staff of music. The notes were tiny butterflies, with a few flying off the organized lines.

He hummed the notes, then sang the accompanying lyrics. It was the line following the chorus near the end of the song. I turned the camera back to me.

"They're perfect. I love them."

"I'll text you a picture of them when we get off the phone. You can tell me if we should go strictly black ink or colors."

"Sounds good. On a different note, did you get my surprise?"

I flipped the phone around to bring the vase of flowers into view. When I turned it back to me, he looked so pleased with himself. "How did you manage to swing this, Mr. Rockstar?"

"Well, I found a florist who could hand dye roses nearby. I placed the order. Then I called your building's doorman and asked if he could put them in your apartment for you as a surprise." He shrugged like it was no big deal.

"You convinced my doorman to go in my apartment?" I was dubious at how he managed to convince my very straight-laced doorman to break the rules.

"Actually, his wife helped me convince him. You

know how charming and convincing I can be to the fairer sex. Mrs. Jones thought I was the sweetest thing," he said smugly and brushed his fingertips against his shoulder.

"You *are* the sweetest thing," I agreed with a laugh. "So, how was your show last night?"

"I'm not too sure. Good I think. Once you got on the plane, I kind of just went through the motions like a zombie. The reviews were good though. It's a good thing I can perform in my sleep." I examined his face on my tiny screen, starved for him. He looked exhausted. When we chatted during my flight, it had been in the middle of the night for him. I should've just let him rest, but even hours after being in his arms, I missed him terribly.

"I miss you too. Is it April yet?" I teased but couldn't muster the smile to back it up.

"Sadly, no. And I hate to cut this short, but I have sound check in five minutes and you look like you could use a nap."

"It looks like you could use one too."

"You'll have to rest enough for both of us at the moment. Duty calls," he said with a grimace.

"I think I totally could sleep enough for two. After a shower to wash the trip off my skin."

"Speaking of showers, you left some of your stuff in my room with my toiletries."

"Probably when I shoved my stuff in your shower basket when we were *conserving* water on the tour bus." I waggled my brows at him.

Laughter erupted from his lips. "Yeah. I have your

shampoo and conditioner. Oh, and your lip gloss and perfume."

"Oh, no. Not my perfume. That's my only bottle of *Happily Ever After*," I whined.

"Don't worry. I'll place an order with Whiff to get you a new bottle on the way," he hastily offered.

"That would be great. Ever since you designed that scent for me, I don't wear anything else. It's like no other aroma fits me anymore." The perfume Dawson designed for me last Christmas instantly became my favorite fragrance.

"It's my favorite scent on you too, well other than mine. It makes you smell like cotton candy. Makes me want to eat you up." He smirked at me as my face heated with desire.

"Hey now, you don't have time to start something right now," I admonished.

He pouted. "Fine. I'll call you after the show. I love you." His fingers stroked the screen.

"I love you too. I'll be counting the minutes. Plug your phone up."

He laughed as he blew me a kiss and disconnected.

∽

Later after a shower and a nap, I woke to my phone chirping.

"Hey, you," I said softly into the camera.

"Hey, baby. It's 3 A.M.," he sang.

🎵 "3 A.M." by Matchbox Twenty

"I must be lonely," I finished the line with a giggle.

"Did you rest?" he asked in his serious voice.

"Yeah. But I'm still jet lagged," I answered with a huge yawn.

"Do you have any photo shoots scheduled tomorrow?"

"No. Thank goodness, I don't have anything for a couple more days." I'd learned a while back that it took me a few days to get back on my own time zone after visiting Dawson on tour.

"Rest up and get back on Eastern Standard Time," he encouraged.

His finger traced the screen of his phone. Closing my eyes, I imagined his touch on my skin. *Damn, I missed it.*

"You're not falling asleep on me, are you?" he teased.

"No. I'm still here. I was just pretending you could reach through the phone to caress my cheek. I know, I know. I'm pathetic." I gave him a weak smile.

"I *wish* I was stroking your cheek. And don't ever talk about the love of my life like that again. She's no more pathetic than I am, skipping out on the after party to come fall asleep on the phone with my girlfriend." He flopped backwards on his bed.

I laughed. "Won't be much of a party without you there."

"Who cares? The other guys eat up all the extra attention."

"Yeah, but Lila wants you to hang out more," I pouted.

"I don't know why. Whenever I show up, I usually sit in the corner talking with some of the instrument techs or roadies. Lila can go screw herself."

"She'd rather screw you, I'm quite certain," I muttered under my breath.

He either didn't hear my comment or he chose to ignore it. "Anyway, our time dealing with her is almost over, baby. And so are these lengthy separations. Next year is all North American stops. And I promise when we're on our own label in eighteen months, I'm going to do what I can to make sure we see each other at least once a month. Either you coming to me, me coming to you, or us meeting in the middle," he swore.

I really hoped he'd be able to make that our reality. It was hard to keep focused on *us*, the longer we were apart.

"Long as we're both coming," I teased, needing to lighten the mood.

His deep chuckle warmed my soul. "We will be. Don't you worry about that... But I *am* serious about how frequently we'll be together. We just have to survive the end of my contract."

"I hope so, Daw. Being with you the past couple of weeks was heaven."

"For me too. And being without you is hell."

"I know." I blinked rapidly, trying to force the tears back. My nose burned with the effort.

"Don't cry. Time will fly. Matter of fact, Steve and Lila gave us our schedule for the next few weeks. It's completely nuts. They didn't even schedule us enough time to sleep. We're doing phone interviews as we drive between venues. So, I'm sorry if I'm more out of touch the next few weeks. I promise I'll text and call when I can."

"Don't worry about me. I'll be here whenever you have time." I longed to ease the guilt evident in his tone. He couldn't help the demands of his job. He was Dawson freaking Anderson, and everyone wanted a piece of him.

"I know. It just makes the whole separation suck more." It was his turn to pout.

"How about we talk about something else?"

"Like what?" he asked.

"I don't know. Something that won't make us sad."

"Then how about we do something else?" His brows waggled suggestively at me.

I licked my lips and nodded. My skin tingled with anticipation of what was to come.

He rubbed his palms against his pants. "Let's switch to our laptops. Be back in two minutes?"

"See you in two." I disconnected.

I hurried to the living room and grabbed my bags. I hadn't bothered to move them further than the entryway when I got home earlier. As I lugged them into the bedroom, I tried to slow my racing heart. My jet lag was taking a backseat to my desires. I tossed my laptop case on the bed, then dug through my suitcase to get my gift. In a few minutes, I had my computer plugged in and perched on the left side of the bed, Dawson's side. A few quick taps connected me back to Dawson's stunning smile and smoldering gaze.

"Ready?" he asked anxiously.

"Mmhmm," I answered. And shifted to a more comfortable position on the bed.

"Hey, did you steal my shirt?"

"Yeah. Sorry. It's new, and it does have *my* slogan on it." I peered down at the words I'd suggested the band use for the latest promotional material. *Loyal to the lyrics, and loyal to the odyssey.*

"It's our best seller at the merch stands. I actually meant to grab one for you in your size. But you kind of distracted me."

"It's a good thing I prefer your shirt to having one of my own." I rubbed my hands across the soft material.

"But it's so big on you." He frowned.

"And it smells like you. When I close my eyes and inhale, I can pretend for a little bit that you're holding me," I confessed.

"Damn, since you put it that way, I don't see how I'm going to ask you to strip naked right now. If I can't touch you directly, at least fabric that touched me can brush against you."

"Well, I'm going to ask you to take yours off. Please," I panted.

He gripped a handful of fabric covering his back and drew it over his head. It was so sexy when he undressed that way. *Who was I kidding?* He was sexy no matter how he stripped. Dawson got to his feet. My mouth went dry as I admired his physique. The muscles of his abdomen rippled as he moved around. His dark jeans hung low on his hips. Reaching out with one finger, I traced the virtual line of those lickable indentations on his pelvis. The edge of his boxers winked at me. He smirked at my expression, as he flicked open the button on his pants. Slowly, he eased the zipper down. With fingers I was desperate to feel on my flesh, he shoved the denim down. A scrap of black cotton followed in its wake.

He let me look my fill before he climbed into bed and tugged the sheet up to his hips.

"Under the covers this time?" I asked in a rasping voice.

"Yeah. I just need to see your face. Focus on the pleasure spilling across your features. Is that OK with you?" He swallowed audibly.

I nodded. Though we'd spent numerous video sessions over the years watching each other writhe with passion, some of our most intimate virtual encounters were under covers. Something about it made it feel more like we were in the same space. I eased my feet to the carpet, wiggling my toes into the soft ply. With a shyness that I rarely felt with Dawson after years together, I chewed my bottom lip and shimmied out of my panties. I inched the hem of his shirt up, briefly giving him a flash.

"Damn," he growled as he leaned toward his computer screen.

I slipped beneath my silk sheet and got comfortable.

"Get your phone and activate the app," he commanded in a gruff voice. He picked up his phone and mirrored my movements on his screen.

"OK," I whispered. "Now what?"

"Turn on your toy." I did as he said while he turned on his.

And beneath the covers with the beauty of technology we set out bringing each other lots and lots of pleasure.

～

A DISTANT CHIME SOUNDED SOMEWHERE. My eyes cracked open, and my head turned, trying to locate the repeating sound. I grabbed my phone where it lay on the unused pillow. The sound wasn't coming from it. It was way too early to be awake. I hadn't willingly seen six in the morning since I finished my coursework. My movements on the bed woke up my opened laptop screen.

It filled with the sleeping form of my love. Long lashes fanned against his cheek. Lips slightly parted, releasing gentle snores. A strong arm wrapped around the pillow I always slept on. A teasing expanse of flesh from shoulder to hip. The muscle flexed. His hips shifted.

🎼 "Hear You Breathe" by Carl Wockner

Then his phone lit up on the bed next to him. *That* was the source of the chiming.

"Baby," my voice was textured with sleepiness. I cleared my throat and spoke again, "Dawson, baby, wake up."

"Mmm." He stirred in his bed, making the sheet slip lower. Bare hip and thigh came into view. *Holy hell.*

"Dawson, wake up. Someone's trying to call you. Incessantly," I urged.

"Am I dreaming?" he mumbled as one eye peeked at me.

"No. But I should still be. It's six in the morning here," I grumbled.

"Then why are you awake? And why am *I*? I was having the most amazing dream. You were here, and we were—"

Before he could finish, his ringing phone was accompanied by a pounding on his door.

"Yo, dude. Lila's been trying to get in touch with you all morning. Answer your damn phone," Brooks shouted through the wood. "And good morning, Izzy."

"Morning, Brooks," I called out. The guys knew Dawson and I always fell asleep on the computer together more times than not.

Dawson picked up his phone and examined the screen.

"What do you think Lila wants?" I asked, not really caring what new offense had her panties in a wad. But I knew he didn't want to have to deal with her.

"Oh, I don't have to think. I have a pretty good idea. She wants to gripe at me about the latest headlines," he mumbled, his eyes trained on his phone.

"What do they say?" I asked, slightly alarmed.

"Don't worry about them right now, flutterby. You

look exhausted. Go back to sleep. I'll deal with this crap." His eyes were sincere.

"OK." I didn't have the energy to argue with him, though tiny part of me wondered what the latest headlines said.

"I love you and will call you later." He blew me a kiss.

"I love you too." I returned the kiss before he closed his computer screen.

My eyes drifted shut, and slumber claimed me again.

Chapter Eight
Dawson

"Dawson, if you're not down here in five minutes, I'm coming in there, regardless of what state of undress you're in," Lila shouted just outside my door.

Growling, I stood from my bed. No point in lingering in it and daydreaming about Izzy. Lila's voice through the pressed wood caused an instant deflation of what dreams of Izzy had inspired. At least I wouldn't have to call Lila back. But she was raining on my parade.

Sighing heavily, I yanked on some clothes. I tucked my phone in the back pocket of my jeans and opened the door. As I plodded barefoot down the stairs, I tugged the hem of my shirt down. Without acknowledging any of the group sitting in the living room, I headed straight for the pot of coffee someone had the good sense to brew this morning. Tipping the pot of heavenly elixir, I filled the mug Izzy made me in the ceramics class she hated. The handle was lopsided, and the rim wasn't perfectly rounded, but I loved it. Once I added cream and sugar, I moved to the couch and sat next to Brooks.

"Where's the fire," Maddox demanded. He looked like he'd just rolled out of bed himself. He didn't come back to the bus when the rest of us did last night, having found a groupie to kill some time with.

"Technically the fire only concerns Dawson. But while you're all here, I need to add a few more things to your schedule."

A collective groan filled the room, which she ignored as she tapped away on her phone. "Let's see, tomorrow in addition to the morning show interview and after party, you also have a photo shoot with *Lady Love* magazine. Then on Friday, we added an interview with *Rock Journey* magazine and a live spot on KROX radio after the concert. And Saturday you have a couple of phone interviews to do while we travel to the next show."

"What the hell, Lila?" I fumed. "Our schedule was already overbooked. When are we supposed to sleep?"

"You guys need to capitalize on the hype. Everyone wants a minute of your time. Be thankful. Give it to them. This could all disappear like that," she said as she snapped her fingers.

"Whatever. We can't perform if we're exhausted. And if we can't perform well, then no one's gonna want to talk to us anyway," Wilder said as he stood and stormed the length of the bus.

"Was that all you needed us for?" Brooks asked, fidgeting in his seat.

"There were a few more additions for next week—"

"Text them all to us," Brooks interrupted as he followed after Wilder.

"Yeah, I'm out too," Jett informed her. Maddox left silently, casting me a pitying glance at leaving me to fend for myself.

I scowled at their retreating backs, but I didn't blame them. If I didn't have to deal with her, I would've been the first one out of here.

Spreading my knees, I leaned back on the couch, adopting a pose of indifference. I didn't speak. Lila moved to the section of sofa I occupied. Once she settled on the cushion beside me, she turned her body toward me, crossing her legs, making her skirt hike up on her leg. She clasped her hands together and leaned forward in a practiced move so that her button-up shirt gaped open.

"You should have the stylist do you up like this for the photo shoot," she said, waving her hand over my body. "Even though you just woke up, you're looking quite hot this morning, or rather afternoon. The women will eat it up."

She'd been quite a bit too forward on more than one occasion. I didn't bother to answer her. My eyebrow quirked up, silently urging her to just get on with it.

She cleared her throat awkwardly. "Anyway, I needed to talk with you about the latest articles. Seems that the images of you and Izzy didn't simply die down." With her bright, red-tipped fingernail, she navigated her phone screen. Once she located what she was looking for, she scooted over next to me on the couch. Her leg brushed against mine. I turned my body, so my knee dug into her thigh, keeping her at bay. With a sigh of annoyance, she handed me her phone.

The headline read, *LO's Dawson Anderson Finds Love*. It contained the two photos which were previously published from Amsterdam. But the article had a new photo. The two of us passionately kissing in the airport. My hand cradled her face, keeping most of her invisible to the camera. The previous photos showed two people enjoying each other's company. But this third photo, though slightly out of focus, showed two people madly in love and saying goodbye.

The article went on to speculate that my absence at parties and clubs was explained by me being in a relationship. The writer thought it was romantic that I'd found love amid the chaos of the music industry. The author also wondered who the girl was who'd captured my heart and put out a call for information.

"You can see the problem," Lila stated.

"Actually, I don't. Unless you mean that people might start harassing Izzy soon. But I *know* that wouldn't bother you. The article doesn't say anything negative about me being in a relationship. It's actually supportive. So, I fail to see what your issue is." I held the phone out to her.

She pushed it back to me. "Look at how many times the article has been shared."

I glanced at it. Ten thousand shares already. "When was this posted?"

"Late last night."

So not even twelve hours old yet.

I whistled. "Wow. It's making the rounds."

"This is *not* something you want to go viral with, Dawson. Check out some of the comments."

She's just a groupie.

She's a prostitute he met in the Red-Light District.

I mean, hello, stripper hair.

I'd bang the unicorn slut.

If Dawson is off the market, what's the point in hanging out after the shows?

That last statement had a lot of interaction beneath it. Some agreeing with the sentiment and others arguing that rockers in relationships would never remain faithful so there was no need to worry.

Fury rose in my veins. *How dare they?* These were supposed to be my fans. They were supposed to care about me.

"You need to let me go public about us. Our real fans will understand. They'll be happy for me."

Lila gave a harsh chuckle. "You didn't read far enough. There are hundreds of comments against you being in a relationship. And do you *really* want people talking about Izzy that way?"

I shook my head. It broke my heart thinking of people saying anything bad about my girl. She was my everything. I had to figure this crap out. "What do you suggest?"

"The same thing I suggested to you a few days ago when your picture hit the papers. Party more. Flirt. Be photographed with girls. Warn Izzy it's coming, so she isn't blindsided." She ticked each item off on her fingers.

"I'll think about it." I didn't want to. But I had to figure out what was the best way to protect Izzy from a situation that looked like it might get ugly.

"You've got to get in front of this. You need this leg of the tour to finish strong. It's only six months. Then you're on a break for a few weeks and won't be in the public eye so much. A lot of important people are watching how the band handles the European and Asian legs of your tour. A lot of people with deep pockets. Movie producers needing soundtracks. Advertising execs needing a catchy jingle. You have to start thinking of all the ways to capitalize on the band's growing popularity."

"Izzy and I will figure out what to do." I stood and moved away from Lila.

"Let me know what you decide, so I can help," she offered as if she was our friend.

I moved down the narrow walkway toward the back of the bus.

"Dawson, don't forget the phone conference with the video director in a couple of hours."

I waved over my shoulder.

∽

LATER THE GUYS and I gathered around my laptop to video conference the director.

"Hey there, fellas," Todd Davidson greeted us.

We returned the sentiment.

"So, I'll just get right to it. According to my notes, your next video is scheduled to be 'Love Rocked'. That's going to be the last single released off your latest album. Right?"

"That's correct," I confirmed.

"I know you guys worked with a different studio on your previous five videos. They were well received by your fans. But I can get you better," he boasted.

We'd all enjoyed working with the other studio and director, but because she was pregnant she was unable to travel to us to shoot the footage.

"What did you have in mind?" Brooks asked.

"Well, if I correctly understand the meaning of the song it pretty much compares love and music."

My lips turned down at his simplistic summation. So many people never bothered to examine the lyrics to the songs that flowed through their ears and into their minds.

He held up his hand and hastened to continue, "I mean, I know it's deeper than that. But the first verse is about loving rock and roll and what music does to your heart. Right?"

"Right," Jett encouraged. The look on his face said he was eager to see what the guy had in mind. Jett was a music video connoisseur.

"And the second verse is about how finding love rocks your heart," Todd continued.

"Mmhmm," Maddox chimed in, his tone noncommittal.

"And the last verse is about how love on the rocks crushes your soul."

"Yeah," I gave him a one-word answer.

"I know your previous videos have pretty much been

live recordings of you guys in concert and the recording studio, but not really telling a story. This song is perfect for telling a story."

I was skeptical. Our previous music videos had been pretty successful and well-received. The fans liked the behind the scenes clips normally scattered within the videos. And those fans who never got the chance to see us in concert, at least felt like it when they watched our videos.

"What is it that you envision?" Wilder asked.

"Well, for verse one, we'll do like you've been doing. Live concert footage. But in addition to filming you guys playing, we'll also put a few actresses in the front row. We film them too. As the verse progresses, you guys will bring them on stage. Lots of sexy dancing from the girls. The song has a sensual beat. It always gets your fans dancing seductively. So, having dancing on stage is a good transition."

The guys were all nodding as he painted an image of what he saw in his mind.

"We're with you so far," Brooks encouraged.

"Verse two, we progress the story. Shots of you guys with the girls from verse one, but more relationship type shots. Flirting. Kissing. Passion. Sex. Well, not actual sex. But implied sex."

"I'm not so sure I'm down with that," I mumbled.

Todd frowned. "When I ran the concept by your manager, the label execs and your PR person, they all thought there would be no issue with you guys getting on board with my vision. This conference call is actually just a formality."

"I just don't know how I feel about pretending to be in a relationship with someone for the video. Our videos before have been authentic. They've been us. This sounds like a lie," I argued.

"It's just acting. We'll hire professionals. They won't get any ideas or anything. You'll have nothing to worry about." He waved off my concerns.

I wasn't supposed to discuss my being in a relationship with anyone. But damnit, I didn't want to kiss some actress. I only wanted to kiss Izzy. The guys looked at me sympathetically.

"Anyway, the third verse will be various versions of breakups. Fights, tears, broken stuff, shouting. You get the idea," Todd continued, completely unaware of the turmoil raging in me. "What do you guys think?"

"It *is* different from our normal. Can we take some time to discuss it and let you know?" I asked.

"Sure. We wouldn't start filming until a couple of months from now anyway. It'll take that long to get everything lined up for where you guys will be then. So, think about it. It could be epic."

"We'll talk about it and let you know. Thanks for trying to develop a concept to fit the song's meaning," Brooks told him before we said our goodbyes and terminated the call.

No one moved once the screen went blank. Wilder cleared his throat. "I kinda like the idea. It goes back to what music videos used to be, a tool to help tell the song's story."

"I get that, man. But I *can't* kiss another girl, act like I'm having sex with another girl, even if it's fake. It would hurt Izzy. Plus, the press is always looking for an opportunity to print trash about me. I don't want to make it easy for them." The very thought of it made me nauseous. I couldn't touch another girl like I was in love with her. I wouldn't. I slammed my fist on the table.

"Maybe the story can be told without you having to take part in that portion of the plot," Brooks suggested.

I nodded in contemplation. "Maybe."

"Talk to Izzy, dude. See what she thinks about the idea," Jett proposed.

"I will. But first I need to talk to her about the damn gossip stories before she finds them on her own."

"Ahh. Is that what had Lila's panties in a bunch this morning?" Maddox joked.

"I don't know anything about Lila's panties. But that *is* what had her so pissy. There's a new article that came out last night showing me kissing Izzy goodbye at the airport."

"Does it have her name?" Brooks asked concerned.

"No. It doesn't even really show her face."

"Oh, well that's not so bad then," Brooks breathed.

"But the comments were brutal. Like ripped her apart brutal. I think Lila just needs to let us go public. She thinks it would be a disaster for ticket sales."

"That's tough. We need to really deliver on this tour

so there won't be any issues with venturing out on our own in eighteen months," Maddox reasoned.

"I know. That's the only reason I haven't declared my love for Izzy on social media already. Made us Facebook official."

"You should talk with her before the show. You know your mind won't be able to settle until you call her," Brooks said.

"You're right. I'm going to go do that now." I stood and tucked my laptop under my arm. Then I strode purposefully back to my room.

With a click of my bedroom door, I shut out the world. Sighing deeply, I flopped back onto my mattress, unable to even smile at the bounce I made. I rolled to my side and booted up my computer. Once I had a search engine up, I did something I hadn't done in years, I typed my own name into the search bar.

The very first result return was the article Lila showed me this morning. In the short time since she'd stormed out, the article had been updated. Now it also included more photos. One of the two of us staring into each other's eyes over a romantic dinner. It was blurry and obviously shot through the window. But Izzy's smile and hair were discernable. The other one was zoomed in on us to the point of it being grainy, but still depicting us floating down the canals in a loving embrace.

How many images were snapped of us without our knowledge? And why did they keep popping up randomly instead of one big expose with the first article released?

It was obvious to anyone looking at the photos, that

we were completely enamored with each other. Lila wasn't going to be able to keep insisting I wasn't in a relationship in her statements to the press. She could deny it and even force me to not confirm it, but the photos didn't lie. The shouted my love, loud and proud.

I pressed the necessary buttons on my phone to video call Izzy.

🎼 "When You're Gone" by Avril Lavigne

When her face filled the screen, the first thing that registered were the dark smudges beneath her eyes. Even her bright smile didn't erase the exhaustion.

"Hey, baby," she enthused, her eyes sparkling.

"Hey there, flutterby. How's your day been so far?"

"Not too bad. I've just kind of hung around the house. Cleaning, painting, you know. Hanging my print of 'Sunflowers' that arrived this morning."

"How does it look?"

"It looks perfect hanging over the couch." She yawned.

"You still feeling jet lagged?" I frowned as I took in the paleness of her skin and the lines around her eyes.

"Yeah. Normally all I need is one long sleep to bounce back. But that didn't quite get it this time. Maybe I'll go to bed early tonight." She brushed off any seriousness that her appearance suggested. "So, what did Lila want earlier?"

"I'm guessing you haven't been surfing the net today?"

"Nope. Why? Is something wrong?" She pursed her lips together.

I exhaled deeply. "Seems we were photographed *several* times while we were out and about in Amsterdam."

"Really? I bet she loved that. Are the pictures bad?" Her eyes rolled.

"No. They did catch us kissing at the airport."

"Hell. I bet that pissed all over her cornflakes. What did the article say?" She leaned to the left, out of the frame of phone's video screen. Soft tapping ensued.

"It said that I'd found love. If you're looking for the article, do *not* read the comments," I warned.

Her face came back into view. "Why not? Your fans hating on me?" she teased.

She had no idea how vicious some of them could be. I hadn't known either. "Something like that," I offered with a shrug.

A muted gasp slipped through her parted lips. "The picture of us in the airport is kind of pretty. I mean it's a bit blurry. But the emotion oozes from the image. I kind of want to save the image to my computer. It's hard to deny that the couple in the photograph is deeply in love," her voice was filled with awe.

"Exactly. I'm kind of relieved in a way that someone managed to capture the depth of our feelings. Makes it hard for Lila to spin it any other way in the press. I don't want people thinking you're some random groupie I picked up after a show."

"I agree. But you know Lila will *never* confirm that you're in a relationship," Izzy scoffed.

"True. But a picture's worth a thousand words, especially when the words are lies."

"How did so many people manage to take pictures of us without us noticing? And how did they always seem to know where we were?" she asked, perplexed. She had a point. It wasn't like we had a trail of people following down behind us. Joe and the security guys were always discreet except when they had to make their presence known.

"I don't know. Maybe because when you're around, the world ceases to exist." I smirked at her, my heart feeling lighter just from being able to see her face.

"So, other than your rude awakening to Lila, how has your day been?" she asked.

The smile dropped off my face. Instantly the heaviness was back, pulling my heart beneath a turbulent sea of worry and fear.

"Dawson, what's wrong? Is everyone OK?" Concern colored her tone.

"Nothing like that," I hastened to assure her. "It's just..."

"Just what?" Her brow furrowed.

"Well, the label hired a new director for our next music video. He wants to go in a different direction from our previous videos."

"Oh. Sometimes different can shake things up. What does he want you to do? Dance around naked? Kill someone? I mean the dread on your face makes it seem like he has envisioned something terrible."

"The song is 'Love Rocked'."

"I love that one. It's so sexy. *You're* so sexy when you perform it." She waggled her brows at me in an attempt to be seductive. It was adorable, which was sexy in its own way.

"It *is* sexy. And that's the vibe the director wants to capture. He wants backup dancers with us for verse one on stage."

"Oh, I could see that. I'm actually surprised the label hasn't made you guys add backup dancers to your shows already. Why does the thought of backup dancers concern you? You're a good dancer, if they make you dance too."

"That's just his vision for the first verse. For the second verse, he wants the backup dancers to enter into on-screen relationships with us."

"Ooo-kaaaay," her voice held a hint of apprehension.

"Yeah. With embraces, kissing, and...." I couldn't even say it. I choked the words down, pushing them away from the tip of my tongue and wishing I could banish the idea of it as easily.

"And what, Dawson?" her voice held an edge of hysteria.

"Implied sex," I mumbled.

She swallowed hard, fighting to figure out how to respond. "I see," she whispered. Her eyes glistened.

"I don't want to do it. I'm hoping they come up with a

way around that part." My eyes begged her to understand.

"And what for verse three?" her voice was so soft.

"Epic breakups."

Her head bobbed. The look on her face shifted, the artist in her envisioning the song being transformed into a work of art telling the story.

"The artist in you is picturing it, aren't you?"

"Yeah. But it's at war with my heart, combatting the part of me that can't imagine the love of my life being immortalized forever with his hands touching another girl. His arms holding another girl. His lips kissing another girl. His flesh pressed against another girl's," her voice broke on the last word.

My heart clenched then lurched like it wanted to jump out of my chest and flee to her. "I know, baby. I don't want it either. I promise, I'm trying to figure out another way."

"I believe you," she whispered and wiped a tear away. "And I know in my head that it would mean nothing. It's just your job. But I still hate it." She straightened her spine. "If you have to do it, I'll find a way to deal with it. Don't worry about me. You're almost done with the record label, so soon you'll be able to call the shots. This is the last video they get a say on."

A lightbulb went off. *Why hadn't I thought of it before?* "Maybe we could get them to use *you* for the video. Then it wouldn't be fake feelings. Well, except for the breakup."

"That's definitely an option. When are they going to shoot the video?"

"In a couple of months," I answered.

"So, when I'm back with you?" her voice was hopeful.

"Possibly. I'll find out for sure." My heart was lighter with the possibility.

"Whatever you find out, don't worry about me or about us. I'll be fine. Anyway, I'm sure it's almost time for you to get to sound check."

I glanced at the time. "How do you do that?" I chuckled.

She smirked at me. "Don't forget to charge your cell phone."

"I won't. Text me when you go to bed."

"OK. Call me after the show."

"How about I text you, and if you're awake still, you can call me back?" I was really concerned by how tired she appeared.

"OK. Have a great show. I love you, baby."

"I love you too, flutterby."

Chapter Nine
Izzy

A couple of days had passed since the photo of me and Dawson saying goodbye was released. I was still exhausted. It was odd. No matter how much I rested, I couldn't quite get my energy levels to replenish. Maybe it was sympathy exhaustion. Dawson was being run more and more ragged with his chaotic schedule.

We talked every chance we could, which wasn't as often as either of us wanted or needed.

Each morning when I woke, it had become my habit to scour the internet for his name to see if there were any new articles about us. We were both worried that it was only a matter of time before someone figured out who I was.

This morning when the search results populated, instead of the first article being about his show a few hours ago, there was a new story about us. Well, about

Dawson and his mystery woman. It had a new image of us. We were wrapped up in each other's arms, kissing in the rain with the canals in the background.

Objectively speaking, I could appreciate the romance of the frozen moment in time. As one of the unwitting subjects, I was a little annoyed that I felt like I had to hold my breath, waiting for the moment when my identity would be revealed. Dawson and I thought it would be better revealing it on our terms, but Lila refused. And unfortunately, she held the power. For now.

Ring. "Hi Mom," I greeted my mom cheerily.

"Hi honey. How are you?" I rested my head back on my pillow.

"I'm good. A little tired, but good."

"So, I'm guessing based on the photos in the media that you enjoyed your trip to Amsterdam?"

I hadn't really checked in with my parents since I'd been back except to text them that I'd returned safely.

"I did, Mom. And I have no idea how so many images were taken of us."

"Honey, Dawson isn't just the boy who grew up next door anymore. He's more than a guy who played his guitar for you to fall asleep by."

"But—"

She cut me off, "I'm not saying that boy isn't still in there. But he's not just *yours* anymore. He's the world's. There's always going to be someone out there watching him, wanting a piece of him. You on his arm means they're watching you too."

"The pictures don't even show my face. And the

press has no idea who I am. I'm halfway around the world now."

"Isabelle, you're a special girl. The world is going to notice you no matter *where* you are. You being with Dawson just catapulted you to that level sooner. Just be careful."

"I will, Mom."

"I love you," she declared.

"I love you too."

When I hung up the phone, I stared at myself in the mirror. Maybe I needed to do something to make myself a little less recognizable. A few people seemed to pay extra attention to me yesterday in the park. It could've just been my paranoia, but my rainbow hair *was* unique. And sadly, it was featuring heavily in the gossip stories about Dawson.

My mind made up, I pulled my hair up into a tight bun, concealing all but the pink. Then I headed to the beauty supply store.

~

Several hours later, I sat at my kitchen counter, eating dinner, chicken stir fry.

Ding, my laptop chimed. Anxiously, I answered the video call—Dawson was supposed to talk with the music video director today.

"Hey, baby," I greeted him when the call connected.

"Hey, you."

I laughed at his image. "Did you take a shower with

all your clothes on?" His hair was flat to his head, and the fabric of his shirt clung to his muscles.

"No. Rainstorm came up during the show. We performed for a little while in it before the powers that be ended the show, worried we'd get sick and be unable to play tomorrow. Or get electrocuted."

"They're probably right. You don't want to catch a cold. If you're sick, then you have to reschedule shows. And the tour lasts longer. You should probably dry off and get warm."

He got to his feet and rolled the damp fabric up his torso. My mouth watered over each inch of flesh unveiled. My fingers itched to trace the dips and valleys of his body. It felt like forever since my fingerprints had been on his flesh. When he peeled the denim off his lower half, my heartrate kicked into high gear.

"You think it will always be like this?" I asked while he vigorously rubbed a towel over his damp skin.

"What do you mean?" His brow furrowed in confusion as he finished whisking the droplets off him.

"I mean, do you think we'll always be this desperate for each other even when we just saw each other a few days ago?"

"Yes," he said simply.

"The master of words only has a one-word answer for me?" I teased to hide my nerves. I always worried that he'd become bored with me or that maintaining a relationship with so many obstacles in the way would become more trouble for him than it was worth.

"I don't need other words. I don't need to explain

how whether I just had you five seconds ago or if five years had passed, I would still want you with every molecule comprising my being, every breath in my lungs, every beat of my heart and every stitch of my soul. There will *never* be a time when I don't want you desperately."

"You sound so sure," I whispered.

"You're not?" He climbed into his bed, beneath the covers.

"I *am* that sure of my feelings. I just know that it would be a lot easier for you to not have to worry about this," I said motioning between us.

"I know Lila made you think that," he started.

I opened my mouth to protest, but he cut me off, "Don't say anything. I can easily imagine what she said to you when you were here. But know this, my life would *not* be easier without you. It would be dark and without a melody. It would be hell. So, I plan to spend every day proving to you that no matter the obstacle, the one thing I'm sure of is our relationship. We're like cockroaches."

He just ruined a beautiful speech. I burst into a fit of giggles. "Did you just compare me to a cockroach?"

"Not exactly. Cockroaches can survive a nuclear explosion or something equally destructive. So, what I mean is our relationship will survive anything that's thrown our way."

"I never imagined that cockroaches could be used in a romantic sense, but somehow you managed to do it."

"I *am* the master of words," he bragged, puffing up his chest like a proud peacock. "Now what did you do to your hair?"

My fingers brushed through my now silvery, purple hair. "Thought I might should change it up from what it was in Amsterdam. I got some looks at the park yesterday when I was doing a shoot there."

"Why didn't you tell me? I can have Joe arrange for someone to be around when you have to go out in public." He leaned forward.

"What? No. I'm just paranoid. Nobody knows my name. And now, I don't even look like the girl in the photos." I did *not* want a shadow when I walked down the street to get a cup of coffee.

"True. It was probably a smart idea to change it up. And I really like that color on you. Who am I kidding? I like every color on you. I'd even like baldness on you," he joked.

"That's not even funny. I'm not going to test that theory out." I shuddered at the thought of having no hair to use for my artistic whims.

"You'd still love me if I was bald, right?" he asked all seriously.

"Hmmm. I do love your hair. It feels so good when I run my fingers through it. And sometimes, I need something to hold on to, so I can guide you to where I need you to be..." I tapped my index finger on my chin, pretending to think it over. "But, I'm pretty sure I'd still love you if you didn't have any hair. I mean, I'd have to use your ears to steer you if you were bald. But I could make it work."

He guffawed loudly. "I'd let you hold on by my ears.

Sometimes the ride gets a little wild." He grinned wickedly at me.

I ran my fingers around the edge of my collar, needing some air.

"Before I forget, I spoke with Todd Davidson today, the director for the music video. It was just the two of us on the call. I asked him if we had to hire professional actresses. He asked me if I had someone in mind. When I told him that I was considering asking my girlfriend to star as my love interest for the video, he wasn't opposed to the idea."

"He wasn't?"

"No, he said so long as we had chemistry on screen, it was fine with him. Now, I know Lila will never get behind it, so I asked him not to mention it to anyone else yet. They'll be in town to do the filming during your next visit, so the timing is perfect." His eyes sparkled at the prospect of shooting the music video together.

"We'll just have to show him our chemistry." I winked and chewed on my bottom lip.

He growled in response. "Exactly. When he sees the two of us together, he'll fight to use you for the video."

His computer and mine both chimed at the same time. "You've been searching your name again?" I teased.

"Yeah. Must be a new article about me. Probably about tonight's show." His mouth said the words, but his face said something different. He didn't think the article was about his upcoming show any more than I did.

I clicked the notification. A small window opened revealing two new stories. One was about how the rain hadn't dampened their performance last night. The other was about us. The photo was of the two of us strolling through the hotel lobby in Amsterdam. The writer speculated that I was an artist because the corner of a sketch peeked out from the top of my bag.

"*Day-uuum*, you look smoking playing in the rain," I cooed, trying to take both our minds off the latest tale about us.

"I hear the worry in your voice. It's OK. There are thousands of artists in the world. That one little nugget of truth isn't going to lead the paps to you."

He knew me so well. "You're right. I just don't want to be ambushed. It's one thing to give information. It's another to have it stolen. And the press is filled with thieves—stealing details, pilfering moments and looting lives. I don't want me or us to be a casualty in their battle for dirt."

"Me either. And I'm going to do everything in my power to make sure that doesn't happen. I'll protect you and us," he vowed vehemently.

I had every confidence that if it was something that he could control, it would be handled. I just wasn't sure that safeguarding us from the paparazzi was within the realm of his command.

We needed a distraction. "How about we read some together now?" I asked, needing the connection to him that came through putting our heads and hearts into the same work of fiction.

"That sounds perfect. Get ready for bed, while I look

at the blurbs, so we can pick." His kindle was already in his hands as he leaned back against his pillows.

I slid off the barstool and carried the laptop with me to my room. "Give me just a minute," I told him as I set the computer on my bed in his spot. I moved around the room—plugging up my laptop so the battery wouldn't die, stripping out of my clothes and putting on a short night gown, powering on my kindle. When everything was ready, I slipped beneath the covers and turned to Dawson.

"What's the verdict?" I asked.

"I vote for *Filthy Beautiful Lies*. I'd love to read the one about the rocker, but I need a break from my own reality right now. That OK with you?"

"Absolutely. I picked the book after all."

Once we loaded the books to our screens, I asked, "Take turns?"

"Always."

And we took turns reading about Sophie and Colton until we were too tired to stay awake anymore.

Chapter Ten
Dawson

Love in an Elevator for LO's frontman, Dawson Anderson was the headline that greeted me when I woke the next afternoon. Staring back from the screen was a photo apparently lifted from the hotel's security camera. I was practically devouring Izzy in the elevator. My hand was gripping her thigh, propping it on my hip, pushing the hem of her dress up. Before I could actually read the information below the steamy image, an alert sounded on my phone.

One word: Dawson.

From Lila.

Tone was impossible to decipher in the written word. But Lila's texts defied that reality. I heard the whining and the scolding in the way she said my name when she was pissed and losing her patience with me. Not that I gave a damn, but her patience with me ran completely out about three articles ago.

Quickly my fingers flew across the screen.

Me: Let me go public.

She didn't even bother to answer. Soon, she'd have no choice. If the trend continued, there would soon be a dozen photos of me and Izzy circulating. Lila and the label could screw themselves.

I shot off a quick text to Izzy, hoping she was still sleeping. She really needed the rest. Between the jet lag and trying to stay on my schedule so we could spend more virtual time together, she was wiped.

Me: We made the news again. We look good. Off to an interview. I love you.

~

Hours later, I was finally done with the interviews and appearances and sound check. I was exhausted, but I had to perform in a couple of hours. I hadn't been able to talk to Izzy all day. It was making me grouchy. Without speaking to the guys, I dashed up to my room. My phone was laying on my bed where I left it. The light was blinking. With a quick swipe, I unlocked the screen.

Izzy: We do look good. Have a great day. I love you.

Later on, was another message.

Izzy: I'm going to bed. I'm so tired. Hope you have a great show. I love you so much.

My heart sank. I hated that I wasn't going to get to hear her voice today. It wouldn't be the first time that we'd had to go twenty-four hours without talking to each other. Hell, we'd even been days a few times. They sucked. But we endured. We made it work. And we'd keep making it work. There was nothing in my life I believed in more than Izzy and me. As long as we had each other, we would conquer everything life threw at us.

Two hours later, I waited by the edge of the stage for the lights to dim. My phone vibrated in my back pocket. I knew I shouldn't look at it. There wasn't time. Our cue should come in thirty seconds. But I couldn't help myself.

Izzy: Sorry I missed your call. I love you. Have a great show. Call when you're done.

Me: About to go on. I love you too.

My heart soared as I slipped the little piece of technology that served as my lifeline when we were apart back into my pocket. Lila walked by. She shot me a glance. It wasn't any of her usual looks—not flirty, not seductive, not arrogant like she knew best. Not even annoyed.

No, this time she looked… triumphant. But I didn't care. Even her presence couldn't rain on my parade at the moment. She'd been oddly absent this evening. Normally, she was everywhere. Maybe she found a job better suited to her where she wouldn't have to annoy the crap out of me. My guitar tech signaled me, preventing me from giving the situation any more thought. I dashed up the stairs into the dark, strapped my guitar around me and took my spot on stage.

When the lights came up, the crowd roared to deafening levels. For two hours, I lost myself in the music, rushing the minutes until I could hear the best song in my ears—Izzy's voice.

Two days later

I woke tangled in my sheets after a crazy night of video chatting with Izzy. Though she still looked a little under the weather, we'd been able to really reconnect. We'd both needed it. The distance was hard. Unbearably hard.

But thanks to Bluetooth technology and some innovative companies in Amsterdam, the oceans and miles between us didn't pose as big of an obstacle as they used to. We both finally passed out after a couple hours of chatting, reading and playing.

I'd still be sleeping if not for the constant chirping of notifications on my computer. That's what I got for leaving it on instead of shutting it down. But it was so worth it to fall asleep staring at her.

I ran my finger across the touchpad to wake it up. Izzy's sleeping form filled the screen. I resized the window of the video so that I could see what was screaming for my attention. As my gaze focused on the screen, I had to blink a few times to convince myself this wasn't a nightmare. I clicked on the first article that popped up. It wasn't a gossip rag, but a legitimate entertainment news site.

Initially all the blood must have fled my brain because I became light-headed. My vision blurred. Starbursts flashed in my peripheral. I closed my eyes and drew in a few deep breaths. When I opened them again, the words were in crystal-clear focus. The headline read, *Dawson + Isabelle = Dizzying Heat*.

Damnit!

They knew Izzy's name.

The article wasn't just some fluff piece. It had Izzy's full name and even said where she was from. It even had a piece of her artwork from a college showing in a small thumbnail image. Even worse than the information were the photos the article had.

Images of the two of us in bathrobes lounging in our hotel suite in Amsterdam.

One of us in the jacuzzi.

Several blurry images of us in bed.

A video clip of us writhing beneath the sheets.

Nothing inappropriate was shown in the photos or the video. But it was obvious to anyone what we were doing.

Rage blinded me to the words on the screen. I didn't know how long I was lost to the tempest of fury swirling inside before a sweet sound acted like a lighthouse beacon guiding me safely to shore. Izzy was calling my name.

Blinking hard, I enlarged the video she occupied. "Hey, baby," she greeted me. She was propped up in bed

—the sheet tucked under her arms, her hair tousled, a beautiful, pink flush on her cheeks. My heart stalled in my chest for half a second.

Her smile chased the largest storm clouds away. "Morning, flutterby. Did you sleep well?"

"I did. Thanks to you. Orgasms are good for the soul. I really needed that. I feel like a new person."

"We *both* needed that. But remember, if you start feeling bad again, you promised you'd go see your doctor."

"I remember. I must not have been sleeping very deeply since I got home. Without you wearing me out, my sleep wasn't restful enough," she said with a laugh. It was music to my ears.

"I'll have to do better then. Thank goodness we have those new toys." I winked at her and licked my lips seductively.

She giggled again. I let the silence marinate between us. I swallowed and tried to figure out how I was going to tell Izzy that not only did the world know her name, but they also knew what her face looked like under a haze of pleasure.

Ringing sounded through the computer. She reached for her phone. "Who would be calling me at this time of day?"

"Don't answer it. Not yet. We need to talk first," I rushed out urgently.

"OK." She set her phone down and looked at me curiously.

"I'm so incredibly sorry, flutterby."

"What for?" Confusion marred her perfect face, creating little lines in her brow.

I just had to say it. Quick. Like ripping off a band-aid. "The press got your name."

"Oh..." Her finger started twisting a strand of hair around it, something she used to do as a kid when she was really nervous. I hadn't seen her do in years.

"Unfortunately, that's not the worst part," I mumbled, my voice filled with a mixture of regret, rage and sorrow.

"What else?" she asked fearfully.

"I don't know how, but they have photos and... uh... a video of us in our room in Amsterdam."

Horror made her jaw drop and her eyes widen. "What kind of pictures?" She was imagining the worst. She knew we were rarely dressed in our room.

I couldn't look her in the eyes. "The worst kind that can be printed in a mainstream publication. Us in robes watching TV. Taking a bubble bath." I filled my lungs with air and blew it out in a rush. "And in bed, making love."

A squeak escaped her lips. Her fingers flew to the keyboard, the motion making the sheet slip lower down her body. I couldn't even let myself appreciate the view. Izzy's life was about to be turned upside down because of me, because of *my* life. Indirectly, I was responsible for the hurt and humiliation she was about to feel.

I didn't have to be on the other side of her screen to know when the webpage finally loaded. Tears leaked from her eyes in a silent stream.

My fingers clenched into a fist, the nails biting into the flesh of my palm. I pounded it into the mattress but found no satisfaction in striking the soft surface. It didn't even make a sound.

"I swear, flutterby, I don't know how this happened. But I *will* get to the bottom of it. Whoever is responsible will pay. In the meantime, I'll get the band's lawyers on it to see what can be done about getting the images down." The fixer in me demanded I take whatever action necessary to eradicate the pain being inflicted on my girl.

The harsh chuckle that erupted from her lips was unfamiliar. Chilling. Aching. "Dawson, you know how the internet works. It's out there now. It will *never* be gone. Everyone in the world knows what I look like when I come now."

Sharp pain stabbed in my chest. "No, they don't, flutterby. I know it's bad. But those images are of the back of your head or your profile. And all the ones from the bedroom are blurry."

"It doesn't matter. They'll fill in the blanks," her voice hiccupped. She looked so broken. So defeated.

"Don't let them win, flutterby. Please," I rasped. "I love you."

"I love you too. Oh my—" Her hand covered her mouth as she jumped from the bed, naked. I appreciated the view for a split second before she disappeared from view. As the computer on her end shook, anxiety ratcheted my heartrate up to unsafe speeds.

Tapping the volume button on my computer, I strained to hear what was going on in the room that held my future. Retching sounds filtered through cyberspace to my anxious ears. The ache in my entire being amplified. She was sick and hurting, and I was a world away, helpless to do anything.

After what felt like an eternity, she came back into view, the band T-shirt she swiped from me on her last visit now engulfing her small frame. Her eyes were red, and her skin was sallow.

"I'm so sorry, flutterby." My trembling fingers brushed against her face on the screen.

"It's not your fault, Daw. I'm not mad at you. I'm mad at the situation. And I'm embarrassed. My parents, my friends, my clients will now see me as part of a sex tape scandal." All celebrities expect to have some sort of scandal at some point during their careers. It was laughingly joked about as a rite of passage in the A-lister circles. But this wasn't the type of thing Izzy signed up for by being with me.

"They know you. It won't make a difference to the people who matter to you," I tried to reassure her.

"Dawson, I need to go," she whispered.

"Don't go, flutterby," I pleaded.

"I have to. I need some time to think." Her face begged me to understand.

"If it gets to be too much... any of this..." I swallowed hard. "...just let me know. I don't want you hurt or uncomfortable or—"

"OK. I promise, I'll let you know." She gave me a small smile of reassurance.

I exhaled loudly. "OK. I'm going to call the lawyer to

see what can be done about getting the photos and video down. There's an expectation of privacy in a hotel room. That has to mean something. And I'll call Steve and Lila, get them to work on preparing a statement. We might officially need to go public now. This may force their hands. If we need to make a joint appearance, I'll arrange everything to get us in the same place for it. And I'm going to call the owner of that hotel too and get to the bottom of who would do something like this. Oh, and I'll get Joe to see what can be done about getting you security so that the paps don't harass you." I was rambling, but she wasn't saying anything. Panic creeped into my soul and squeezed it in a vice.

"Hold off on the bodyguard thing. I changed my hair. I'll be less noticeable this way. Having a big guy following me around will just draw attention back to me," she reasoned.

"I'll just get things in place in case you do need it. OK? It'll make me feel better. Please?" I gave her my puppy dog eyes. She'd never said no to them before.

"OK," she relented. "I love you."

The noose around my heart loosened a little. It wasn't that I doubted her love, but the reassurance those three words gave me... there were no words to describe it. "Oh flutterby, I love you too. So damn much. This is just a bump in the road. We'll figure things out."

She nodded. "I'll call you later, OK?"

I swallowed hard. "If you don't get me, I'll call you back. I don't know what this latest news does for all the appearances the band is supposed to have today."

"I'm sure Lila will capitalize on the increased publicity. But she'll want you to spin it some way that fits the label's image needs for you."

I sighed heavily. She was right. Lila and the label probably wouldn't let me be honest about our relationship.

"Screw what they think. I should just tell the first person who asks me about it that I'm in love with you and have been for almost two decades."

Her face lit at my impassioned vow. "You know you have to do what they want. You're under contract for a while longer. You can't throw away your future. We'll figure things out."

I nodded. "You're right. I'll see what they say first. And I'll let you know if there's anything they want you to do."

"OK. I'm going go for now. We've both got stuff to figure out and deal with." She tucked her hair behind her ears and offered me the tiniest of smiles.

I nodded. "I love you. No matter what the next few days hold, don't forget it," my tone was impassioned.

"I won't. And don't you forget how much I love you, Dawson Anderson." A fierceness flared in her green eyes.

The screen faded to black as she blew me a kiss and disconnected.

Something inside of me cracked and sank like a rock. But I didn't have time to dwell on it. I texted Steve and Lila. I didn't waste words on pleasantries.

Me: Fix it. I don't care how. Get the pictures and video down.

Me: And warn everyone who wants an interview, I'm NOT talking about my relationship with Izzy.

I didn't wait for a response. I dialed Joe.

"Hey, D. I saw," he said immediately.

"Then you know why I'm calling." I was grateful I wouldn't have to explain everything to him.

"You want someone on Izzy." It was a statement, not a question.

"Yeah. But she doesn't want it unless it's absolutely necessary." I ran my fingers through my hair, tugging hard on the strands.

"I'm on it already. Don't worry. We won't let anything happen to her."

"Thanks."

I disconnected and dialed the lawyer.

∽

Hours later, I had no answers as to who was responsible. Joe sent one of his guys back to the hotel in Amsterdam to look for the cameras in the suite. It was a long shot. Whoever planted them probably retrieved them after we checked out. But I'd feel better knowing that no one else would be violated like we were.

The hotel owner called me directly before I could call him. He was in the process of interrogating his staff and promised to keep me informed of what he found out. But everyone who'd been assigned to care for us and our suite had been employed by the hotel for years. And they were used to taking care of celebrities. Nothing like this had ever happened before.

The lawyer assured me that he would get the legitimate sites to take down the photos and videos, as we weren't out in public. But he also reinforced what Izzy said—the internet was forever. A bell couldn't be unrung. The photos were out there. They'd always be out there.

Internally, I vowed to pay someone to scour the world wide web everyday and send takedown notices to the sites publishing the photos and video of us from our suite. Eventually, the vultures would find a new carcass to devour. In the meantime, I would do what I could to minimize the flesh available for them to chew on. Especially Izzy's.

When I finished the calls, I had several unread text messages.

Dad: Saw the news. You OK?
Me: Trying to fix things now.

Mom: Sweetie, how did this happen? Is Izzy OK?
Me: Trying to deal with things. Will talk to you later.

. . .

Izzy: I LOVE you. Just wanted you to know that. XOXO

Me: I love you too. Hang in here with me.

Dragon Lady: You will be VAGUE in all interviews. You do NOT have to deny a relationship. But under no circumstances are you to confirm one either. Instruct Izzy to not comment if she is approached.

I didn't bother to reply. Instead, I messaged Izzy.

Me: Lila says that I am to be vague about our status.

Izzy: Did her highness have instructions for me?

Me: Yeah. Don't comment.

Izzy: Got it. Have a great show.

Me: That's the farthest thing from my mind. I wish I could cancel it.

Me: Are your parents freaking out?

Izzy: Yes. They want me to come home until this dies down.

Me: Might not be a bad idea.

Izzy: Maybe. But only if it gets nuts here. I have work to do.

Me: Be safe.

Me: Please. I don't want anything to happen to you.

Izzy: I will. I'm not going anywhere today. I don't feel well.

Me: Soup for dinner. Then bed for you.

Izzy: Don't have any soup. But I'll figure something out.

I TYPED the name of her favorite diner into the search engine on my laptop. A few minutes and a hundred-dollar tip later, Izzy's favorite soup and grilled cheese were on the way to her house.

Me: Soup and sandwich are on the way.

Izzy: ??

Me: I called Faye's and ordered it for you.

Izzy: They don't deliver.

Me: They do for me. ;)

Izzy: Even on the other side of the Earth, you're taking care of me. XOXO

Me: I'll always take care of you.

Me: I have to go now. TV appearance.

Izzy: I love you. Good luck.

Me: I love you too.

By the time I was back in my room on the bus, I'd surpassed exhaustion. Thank God for muscle memory. It was the only thing that got me through the past few hours. I was on autopilot.

Smile. Shake hands. Grit teeth. Answer questions about our music. Dodge questions about Izzy and our relationship.

Drive to venue.

Smile. Say hi. Sign autographs. Repeat a few dozen times.

Walk on stage. Pluck the strings. Belt out the lyrics. Dance. Smile. Repeat for fifteen songs.

Run off stage. Wait. Return. Perform two encores.

Shower. Dress.

Smile. Say hi. Sign autographs. Repeat too many times to count.

Finally, return to my bed, alone and desperate for her voice.

Chapter Eleven
Izzy

The first week after the pictures were printed, I didn't even leave my apartment. A couple of reporters were noticed by the doorman and ran off a couple of days after the story broke.

At least now the reporters were finally convinced that I didn't actually live in my building, so they stopped camping out across the street. But just to be safe Dawson arranged to have groceries delivered to me. And I rescheduled all my photo shoots for next month. Instead, I devoted my time to working on the band images from my visit. The edited images would be delivered ahead of schedule. Maybe that would please Princess Pissy.

Ten days after my name and sex life became fodder for the masses, the paps finally found out my phone number and started calling. Everyday. All hours of the day. Everyone wanted a comment or an interview. I was exhausted, irritated and miserable.

I needed to hear Dawson's voice. His schedule had been impossible, so we hadn't talked recently. I dialed his number. When his voice came through on the other end of the phone, it was in the form of his voicemail greeting.

After the beep, I took a deep breath and started talking, "It's been a few days, baby. I bet you lost your phone charger. The press found out my number. The nerve of some people. Anyway, just wanted to let you know I love you, and I got a new number so that the reporters can't harass me too much. I'll text it to you when I hang up. My old number will only work another few hours. Talk to you soon. And don't worry, we'll get through this. A bunch of nosey reporters don't scare me."

I wanted him to know that I wasn't wavering in my commitment to us even though things were impossibly difficult at the moment.

I texted him my new number

Emotions rioted in me. I didn't know which end was up. I couldn't even name all the things I was feeling. So, I did what I always did when life got overwhelming. I painted my feelings—bleeding my fears, feelings and worries onto canvas after canvas. I was lost. Without connecting with my anchor, I was floating adrift.

Desperate to connect with him, I grabbed the jar of tiny paper stars from my nightstand. Twisting the top, I opened the container. With my eyes closed, I reached in and pulled out a star. I ran my fingernail under the tiny edge to free the tucked end. In seconds, I had the strip unfolded and smoothed flat.

You are the sunshine in my darkened world. I love you.

I smiled. The message was just what I needed.

I decided to shoot him a text in case he couldn't answer his phone wherever he was.

Me: You're my sunshine too.
Me: Did you lose your phone?
Me: Love you.

I tried not to keep track of how long it had been since I'd heard his voice or seen his face. We'd survived a few days without talking before.

His schedule got even more insane after the photos released, and it was already nuts. People who hadn't shown interest in the band, now suddenly vied for a minute of their time. I tried to be excited for him and supportive.

After the first TV interview, I stopped watching them. I couldn't take it. My heart leaped at seeing him, but it quickly crashed when he had to sit there and deny our love. That first interview, he did exactly what the label wanted...

"Dawson, I know the question on everybody's mind is are you in fact in a relationship with Isabelle?" the morning show host with the bleached white smile asked.

Dawson's body stiffened. "Pat, you've interviewed how many young rock stars over the years?"

"Umm... Maybe a hundred?"

"And how many young rockers with hot women willing and available in every city are in relationships?"

Pat mulled it over for a few silent moments. "None that I can recall."

"Need I say more? Now how about we talk about what really matters, like the single we're going to be dropping in a few weeks?"

My heart still hurt over the memory of his mention of all the women who were ready to jump in his bed. I told him to do what the label recommended. But it still wounded me deeply when he was ambiguous about our relationship. He hoped without his confirmation, the story would die, and the reporters would leave me alone.

~

I had to do something to get myself out of this funk. Maybe a bubble bath would cheer me up. I moved woodenly to the bathroom and turned on the water, so it would get hot. Then I opened the cabinet under the sink to find my favorite bottle of bubble bath. As I rooted around in there, my gaze landed on something that stopped my heart. I fell to my butt and yanked out the box. With trembling fingers, I pulled my phone from my pocket and opened the calendar. Rapidly, I scrolled backwards, mentally calculating.

That explained a lot. Fumbling for the faucet, I shut off the water. I pressed the necessary buttons to call Dawson. His voicemail picked up immediately. Guess I was leaving another message.

"Hey baby. I hope things are OK. I need to talk to you about how to handle something. Call me back. I love you."

I opened my internet browser for the first time in a few days. After confirming my suspicions through a Google search, I knew what I had to do.

I shot a text off to Dawson.

Me: Whenever you get this, call me right away. It's important.

Somehow, I got dressed, tucking my hair up in a beanie, and left my apartment for the first time this week. With my head down, I made my way to the closest store a few blocks away.

～

As far as I could tell, my twenty minutes outside the sanctuary of my apartment went unnoticed. Back inside, I made my way to the bathroom. Pulling the boxes from my shopping bag, I lined all seven of them up on the counter. The clerk had given me a weird look when I plopped so many on the checkout stand. But there had been too many options. And rather than debating which was the most accurate, I bought them all.

I sucked in a deep breath and popped open the end of the first box to remove the instructions. I scanned the sheet of paper several times. There was no way that something with the potential for holding life-altering answers should be so simple to take.

Oh well, that's why I bought a bunch. In case I messed up.

Two minutes later, I was pacing my bedroom, cataloging my symptoms, which Google had so graciously provided me. Tiredness. Achiness. Moodiness. Nausea. Dizziness.

I was scared. But I remembered what Dawson told me during my visit. The words brought comfort as I replayed them in my mind. He would want to be part of this moment.

I dialed his number again, hoping to get him before I went back in the bathroom. Voicemail again.

"Dawson, call me as soon as you get this. I'm scared. I think I'm... never mind. Just call me back."

Crap. In my anxiousness I forgot to tell him I loved him. I pressed the screen again. I listened to the voice I loved again, then waited for the beep. "Forgot to say, I love you."

I'd have to look at the results without him. Straightening my spine, I marched into the bathroom, fully prepared for two pink lines.

When I picked up the stick and peeked in the window, only one line stared back at me. Frowning, I put it back down and double checked the instructions. The test said negative. I must have done something wrong.

Going to the kitchen, I grabbed a bottle of water and downed it quickly. I forced my brain to think about water and rain and waterfalls and waves, anything to generate the urge to pee.

This time I peed in a cup. Then I dipped an applicator from each box into the cup. And waited.

And waited.

And waited some more. I'd decided to give them an extra minute for good measure.

When the time was up, I carefully examined all six of them. Negative, negative, negative, N pregnant, negative, negative.

Maybe they were false negatives. Time for more Google.

The helpful entity that the search engine was, informed me that first urine was best. So, I needed to pee on them first thing in the morning. I'd need to survive the next ten hours without confirmation.

I stood in front of the mirror on my closet door and ran my hand across my abdomen, imagining a perfect combination of me and Dawson already safely growing inside of me.

As scared as I was, the thought filled my heart with joy and love that I hadn't expected.

With a happier heart, I opened my email, deciding to try that mode of communication.

. . .

To: Daw

Subject: Love You

Dawson, I left you a voicemail, but I know you forget to charge your phone all the time when you're on tour. I hope you're checking your email. Something's wrong. We weren't exactly careful when I came out to visit. You know with me forgetting to take a few pills because of the time differences and excitement. So, I'm not blaming you or anything. I took a few tests, and they're all negative. But all the symptoms fit. And so, does the timing. It explains my exhaustion. I'm going to make an appointment to see a Dr. in a few days. Just wanted you to know what's going on. Call me as soon as you get this. We can figure things out together. I need you. Please call me or write or text. Don't forget I changed my number. I love you.

I'D CALL my doctor's office in the morning. I'd continued to take my birth control pills this whole time. So, I needed to make sure everything was OK with the baby IF I was pregnant.

Chapter Twelve
Izzy

Next day...

Me: I know you're OK. I saw an interview you did this morning. Why aren't you calling me back?

Hours later...

Me: Did I do something wrong?

Chapter Thirteen
Izzy

Next day...

Me: Did the label tell you to distance yourself from me?

Chapter Fourteen
Izzy

Next day...

When my text messages still went unanswered, I tried to call him again.

"Since you aren't answering your phone or text messages, I'll try to email you again."

Chapter Fifteen
Izzy

Next day...

After I got home from the doctor's office, I walked around in a daze. I couldn't wrap my mind around the possibilities. I was so scared. There was only one thing I could do. I picked up the phone.

"Dawson, I need you. Please call me back." I tried so hard to make my voice sound strong. To force it not to crack. He promised he'd always be here for me. I'd never needed him more.

🎼 "More Than Words Can Say" by Alias

Chapter Sixteen
Izzy

Three days later...

I was on my own. The sooner I faced it, the better off I'd be.

Me: I'm going to back off. I've got other things I need to focus on. I love you.

Shattered bulbs can't give off light. A broken clock can't measure time. A shattered mirror can't reflect the truth. A broken car can't get from point A to point B.

How does a broken, shattered heart still beat? Why is it still expected to keep us alive?

Chapter Seventeen
Izzy

Two days later...

To: Dawson
Subject: OK

Dawson, I never heard back from you. I guess you're too busy. Just wanted to say I miss you, and if you still want to check in that's OK, but if you don't, I'll be fine. Everything is sorting itself out. Love you.

Chapter Eighteen
Izzy

A week later...

My beautiful roses had finally given up their color and drive for life. Maybe it was time for me to give up too. I pulled one of the dry, drooping blooms from the vase and tucked it into a bud vase. I threw the rest of the bouquet out.

Flipping through the pages of my sketchbook, I found the beautiful vibrant bloom I'd drawn a few weeks ago when I'd come home with a heart full of love and happiness. I set the bud vase on my desk in a shaft of sunlight. Then I propped the sketchpad up next to it. My mind worked, merging the two into one vision. I prepared my palette and sat in front of a blank canvas. As tears coursed unchecked down my cheeks, I painted a rose—

drooped over, crying the colors from its petals into a puddle surrounding the vase.

I spent all day at my easel. When I was done, I stepped back and admired the symbol of eighteen years of love now faded and brittle. I took out my phone and tapped out a text message.

Me: Guess you decided that a relationship wasn't what you wanted after all. I wasn't what you wanted. Goodbye Dawson. Have a nice life.

Chapter Nineteen
Izzy

A week later...

The paparazzi had given up on me, so I could leave my house without constantly glancing over my shoulder. Last week was the first time Dawson wasn't the primary headline on the major websites. I could finally go online without his face taunting me, cracking my heart further.

Feeling safe, I opened a web browser. I needed to email a client the proofs of her session. When Yahoo finally opened, the face that had been haunting my dreams was front and center. Well not his full face. Most of it was blocked by some dark-haired girl sucking face with Dawson on the couch of his bus. Tears filled my eyes as I clutched my stomach.

The headline screamed *LO Frontman definitely back on the market, or maybe was never off it.*

The rest of the article blurred in the haze of my tears.

I clicked the email icon. Rage and fury and agony overruled all my good sense. Angrily, I stabbed the keys.

To: Dawson

Subject: WTH

What the hell is this article talking about? Maybe that's the answer you've been trying to tell me with your silence. *A picture's worth a thousand words, especially when the words are lies.* You said so yourself.

I'm sorry I didn't get the message sooner. I won't bother you anymore. Good luck with everything.

~Izzy

Then I attached the article and hit send.

🎝 "Broken" by Lifehouse

I moved to my sanctuary, the spare bedroom set up as my art studio. I sank down at my desk and found a blank page in my sketch pad.

With tears blurring my vision, I began sketching what was in my heart. Sure strokes with my colored pencils created the face I'd loved for as long as I understood what love was. A face that now brought me unbelievable heartache. I had to get him out of my system the only way I knew how. I moved to the right side of the page and drew my own face, gazing at him with all the love one heart could hold. Our expressions were serious, loving, broken.

Tears shimmered in both our eyes. Then I added our hands, gently cupping each other's cheeks. They could've been holding on or letting go. It was unclear in the sketch.

Without marring the life-like detail, I drew a jagged line—a symbolic rip—right down the middle, separating us on paper much like we were now forever separated in reality.

Drawing a deep breath, I leaned back to examine my work. It was beautiful. It was heartbreaking. It was perfect. Just what I needed to do for myself.

On a pink Post-It, I scribbled: One final memory to add to your sketchbook.

I stuck it to the top of the sketch. Stared at the colors, the lines, the technique. Tried to detach myself from the subject. To view it critically. I couldn't. It hurt too much.

This image would complete our story. Stamp *"the end"* on it in the sketchbook I'd given him back when he moved away after sixth grade. I'd been adding to it over the years, illustrating the story of us. All stories had an ending. This was ours.

I opened the bottom drawer and pulled out two pieces of thick cardboard. Using them, I sandwiched the sketch safely between them. Carefully, I slipped the protected sketch into a padded envelope. I wrote the address of Dawson's apartment in LA on it.

I'd mail it tomorrow. I was too tired now.

Treading down the hall with heavy steps, I went in my room. One look at the bed I'd shared so many moments with Dawson on, laughing, loving, talking, sharing, living—in person and virtually—and I began to tremble with the effort to hold back my wails. I couldn't sleep in there.

I snatched my pillow off my bed and tugged a blanket out of the closet. I sank onto the couch and prayed for sleep to come quickly.

Chapter Twenty
Izzy

I woke on the couch. My eyes ached, my neck was stiff, my heart hurt. As I tossed and turned on the couch last night, waiting for slumber to claim me, I figured out a plan of action. It was what I had to do in order to close the Dawson chapters of my life.

Systematically, I moved around my apartment, taking down photos and mementos, emptying drawers of band T-shirts and boxing up all the tokens of our relationship. The *Sunflowers* reprint came off the wall. The jar of wishing stars removed from my nightstand. Marching to the kitchen, I pried the magnets from our bucket list stops off the refrigerator door. Then I grabbed a large trash bag. I couldn't dwell on this anymore. I had more important things that needed to occupy my mind. There was no room for heartache. Not now.

Holding the bag open with one hand, I picked up the

box of photos, scrapbooks and songs. The box hovered in my grasp over the gaping hole of the trash bag.

But I couldn't let it go. Weeping, I carried the items into my closet. I climbed up on the stepstool and shoved everything into the far, dark corner. I could throw it out later. When I was stronger.

I collapsed on the bed sobbing uncontrollably. My phone chimed with an alert.

The sender was unknown. I should've ignored it. But no one had my new number. Curiosity always killed the cat.

Unknown: You get to see the first cut.

A video attachment followed. I opened it. The opening strains of "Love Rocked" blared through the tiny speaker. The new music video. They must have shot it early. Without me.

The camera zoomed in on Dawson as he sang the opening lines. As it panned back out, a girl with dark, curly hair started dancing around him, trailing her hands across his body and his guitar. I paused it, staring at the girl. It looked like the girl he was photographed with. I deleted the message without watching the rest of the video.

🎼 "Where Do Broken Hearts Go" by Whitney Houston

THE END (for now)

Note from the author

Thank you so much for taking a chance on a new author. As a reader, I know just how many book options are out there for you to spend your time and money on. It means a lot that you gave me a chance. I'd love to hear from you about what you thought of the first installment of Dawson and Izzy's story.

I want to explain how this story came to be. One night as I was trying to go to sleep, a new character started speaking to me in the form of a letter. It was Izzy. You can read her letter in the sneak peek in the following pages. So, I immediately set out writing Dawson and Izzy's story, putting my other book on hold. This second chance romance was destined to be my debut novel. That book is currently being written and is about seventy-five percent done. While I was writing it, I had this brilliant idea to write a short story to let my newsletter subscribers get a glimpse of Dawson and Izzy's first try at love and its end. As I wrote, the short story that was supposed to just be ten thousand words kept growing. By the time it hit forty thousand words, I knew I needed to regroup on my plan. That is how you came to be reading *Beats of the Heart*.

Sneak Peek

Want to find out what happens with Dawson and Izzy next? Their story continues in *Notes of the Heart*. Sign up for my newsletter to find out when the next installment will be available.

Notes of the Heart
Blurb:
Their hearts were in harmony… until the music faded away.

Izzy

Best friends to soul mates to … nothing. Since we were six, Dawson was the most important person in my life. He was my first everything. First friend, first boyfriend, first kiss, first love, first *time*, first heartbreak.

For years our love was a masterpiece. Then two years ago, he ghosted me. Now my world is grey. I'm finally trying to start over, to add muted colors back. Beckett has my trust and friendship, but what he wants most I can't give him, even if I owe it to him. Every time I try an old song resurfaces and starts singing a familiar tune.

Dawson

Now I know why they call it *falling* in love. The splat at the end. I should've known better than to fall for my best friend. Because now I've lost my love, my friend and the inspiration for every song I wrote. My dreams are my reality, and I have it all, except the one thing I want: Izzy. Every song I perform is a reminder of what she inspired. Without her, the music that used to flow freely has died. If I can convince her to be my song, my everything once more, then maybe I won't feel so out of tune. But her heart's singing a new melody, and I may be too late.

Can Dawson make Izzy see the classic anthem is better than a one hit wonder?

Excerpt from Notes of the Heart

Hey you,

Yeah, I mean you reading this letter. Sorry for the informal address, but I don't know you, so that's the best I've got. I know I must sound crazy. Maybe I am. I don't know what's crazier, me actually writing a letter instead of texting, tweeting and posting some passive-aggressive message on Facebook or me reaching out to a stranger thinking you might hold the answers to help me.

I figure this whole mess started with a letter, well a drawing mostly, that he answered. Then it ended with a letter he didn't, so maybe a letter can help me find clarity. Maybe I should start at the beginning. Then after you have all the facts you can tell me what to do.

When I was six, I needed a friend. So, I drew a picture and asked him. He said yes.

When I was eight, I wanted a boyfriend. So, I wrote a note and asked him. He said yes.

When I was sixteen, I needed a prom date. So, I sent an email and asked him. He said yes.

When I was twenty-one, I wanted an opportunity. So, I sent a text and asked him. He said yes.

When I was twenty-three, I needed him. So, I called. He didn't answer. So, I sent a text and an email and a note and a picture. He never answered.

Now, I'm twenty-five, and I need to move on. I need to live and love and be happy. He's living his dream and loving life somewhere else. I have a second chance at life, and I need to take it.

But today there was an envelope in my mailbox. That old familiar handwriting that I haven't seen in years, well other than all the times I dig through my box of memories hidden in my closet. Maybe I should just throw it out with all the junk mail that also filled my mailbox and pretend I didn't see it like he did all those years ago with my messages. What do you think?

Thanks,
Indulging in Idiocy (aka Izzy)

Dear Universe,

I'm an idiot. Words have always mattered to me, whether they were scratched in childish scrawl with a crayon underneath a drawing or written in beginner's cursive in a note passed in class or inscribed in a beautiful looping script within a sketchbook or shorthand text speak or quick messages of encouragement in my inbox or etched on my heart forming a song. They've always come easily, even when I don't let them out. But for the first time in my life, I think words may fail me. I don't know what to do. It's my hope that if I share some of them with you, you can help me find the right ones to regain what I've lost. I swear I'm not nuts. I'm just a man who loved a girl, and then like an idiot left her behind to chase my own dreams. But even the brightest of dreams coming true lose their sparkle without someone to share them with. Without *the one* to share them with. I need to go back to the beginning, back to when it all started with a note.

When I was six, I was lonely. Until she became my best friend.

When I was nine, I was miserable. Until she became my refuge.

When I was eleven, I was lost. Until she became my song.

When I was sixteen, I was in hell. Until she became my heaven.

Sneak Peek

When I was nineteen, I was falling. Until she became my rope.

When I was twenty-one, I was soaring. Until she became my anchor.

When I was twenty-three, I was a star and, on my way, to having it all. Until it all became a black hole with no sun in sight.

Now, I'm twenty-five, and I'm lonely and miserable and lost and in hell and falling. And I'll continue being all those things until I either crash and burn or... Until I convince her to be my anchor, my rope, my song, my refuge, my best friend, my everything once more.

What do you think? Can I win her back? I know I don't deserve her back in my life. She was always there for me when I needed her. And I didn't return the favor. What should I do? She has a chance at happiness. Can I stand in the way of that?

Sincerely,

Dying in my Dreams (aka Dawson)

About the Author

So, I know these things are generally written in third person as if someone else is talking about me. But I just can't do it. LOL. It may be "unprofessional" but I'm just me. And I hope that's OK with you guys.

I'm a Carolina girl, through and through. I have lived in North Carolina my whole life. I'm a wife, a mom, a scientist and a freelance editor. And I'm really hoping to add author to the list.

For as long as I can remember, reading has been my favorite way to pass the time. I always have a book with me and usually am reading more than one at any given time. Editing for indie authors gave me a unique glimpse into the indie publishing world. It's a world I'm really enjoying becoming a part of.

I'd love to hear from you guys. Tell me what you think of Dawson and Izzy. Recommend a great book for me to check out. Let me know what typos you found within my pages. Whatever you want, I want to hear from you.

Newsletter: http://eepurl.com/dBkmHL

Website: https://charlirosewriter.wixsite.com/website

Email: charlirose@charlirosewriter.com

My reader group: Charli's Rockin' Reader group: https://www.facebook.com/groups/248156682622380/

Acknowledgements

Wow. I never imagined I would be doing something like this. Writing was never really on my radar until a couple of years ago. It's been a long process, and I've learned it really does take a village to do something like write and publish a book. I'm going to do my best to thank everyone in my village. If I miss someone, it isn't because you aren't important. It's because the list is monstrous.

First to my husband, Brian, who has always encouraged me in any endeavor I decided to undertake, thanks isn't enough. You're the inspiration to every romantic thing that pops in my mind. And to my son, Matthew, for being quite understanding when work for Mommy seems to never end, I love you.

Thank you, Leslie, for being by my side for nearly three decades, loving and encouraging me and offering your expertise on all things art related in this story. Your willingness to read and give honest feedback as I went was invaluable. And thank you to Leslie's other half, CJ for your help on the music side of things.

Thanks to Alora for starting my feet moving down

this path with a shove of encouragement after a brainstorming session for *your* books. And thanks to you and your daughter, Elora for your help with the photo edits for the cover. The dye job on Izzy's hair turned out better than I ever expected.

Susan, thank you first of all for giving a beautiful face to this story. It is stunning. But more than that, thank you for your friendship and support. I've needed it *so* many times to keep putting words to paper. Without you, I probably would've let this thing sit in my computer forever.

Krysta, Yanette, Keshia, and Ambere, you all have been wonderful with giving advice, feedback, encouragement, and friendship, never once worrying about how I would be able to juggle polishing your words while writing my own.

Ann Marie, your friendship and wisdom were vital during this experience.

Tempi, you've been amazing in the short time I've known you. It's rare for someone to be so willing to help a new friend so much. Thank you.

Jill, thank you for reading my unpolished words for me. Your reassurance and friendship mean the world to me.

Athena, Crystal, Anne, Kennedy - thank you all for inspiring me and encouraging me to pursue this dream.

Rebecca and Heather, thank you both for pushing me to write my best version of this story. I can't even begin to thank you for your ability to drive me to be better.

Nathanie, thank you so much for not only polishing

my words, but also loving my characters and worrying about them.

Special thanks to two authors who were willing to allow Dawson and Izzy "read" their books as a way to stay connected while they were apart. As a reader myself, I highly recommend the books. Cassia Leo's *Shattered Hearts Series* https://amzn.to/2z2as1H and Kendall Ryan's *Filthy Beautiful Lies* https://amzn.to/2ywf2Ws are both great reads and some of the first books I ever read when I got my first Kindle. Also, thanks to Crystal Kaswell for letting her tattoo shop make a cameo. If you enjoy sexy tattoo artists, check out her *Inked Hearts Series* https://amzn.to/2D41wgv

Thank you to Whiff for helping me create something unique. Izzy's special perfume mentioned in the book is an actual perfume that I worked with a perfumer to design. It really is called *Happily Ever After*, and it is amazing. If you want your own bottle of it, here's the link to it https://www.whiff.com/products/charli-happily-ever-after

And to everyone who took a chance on an unknown author, thank you. Knowing that you took the time to read my words is truly humbling. I hope you'll reach out and let me know what you thought. And I really hope you'll tune in for the next chapter in Dawson and Izzy's love story. If you enjoyed *Beats of the Heart*, please consider leaving a review on Amazon for it.

CPSIA information can be obtained
at www.ICGtesting.com
Printed in the USA
LVHW091521051118
596005LV00001B/169/P